AMERICAN DEMOCALYPSE
UNCIVIL WAR
BY
PATRICK BRYAN TAYLOR

ISBN: 978-0-578-34749-3

Cover design by Justin Tolbertson

DEDICATION

For every citizen of the world that believes
America is not a place to be surrounded by
walls, but an Idea that can bridge the divide and
unite us as humankind.

ABOUT THE AUTHOR

Patrick Bryan Taylor developed a deep interest in our American government and the U.S. Constitution as a child. Thanks to some very influential social science teachers, that interest became an obsession. After graduating from high school, he enlisted in the U.S. Navy, where he first served as an Electronic Warfare Technician and later as a Cryptologic Technician, advancing to the rank of Chief Petty Officer.

Patrick spent several years as a volunteer in his local communities, mentoring and counseling unaccompanied homeless and at-risk youth. He also trained volunteers, led street outreach counseling teams, and served as a local community Executive Director. After leaving the Navy, he decided to transition into the field of education, where he spent a few years educating youth about civics and our democratic society. He left that field to pursue his passion of working in the LGBTQ+ community, where he now empowers LGBTQ+ youth to improve their lives and enable them to be the next generation of leaders. He recently moved to Arizona where he lives with his husband and daughter. This is his second book.

TABLE OF CONTENTS

INTRODUCTION

If you have ever felt concerned about the sustainability of our nation's democratic way of life, then this is the book for you. This is the second book in the series. When I wrote the first book, *Tyrant: Dividing America*, it was meant to be a single book, rather than a series. It began as a sequential series of dreams from anxiety I had about the upcoming 2020 presidential election. I developed a great concern that the president would not leave office peacefully had he lost the election.

I wrote my dreams down in a journal. Each dream seemed to pick up where the last one ended. At first it seemed impossible, but eventually what I wrote began to seem more likely. After reading through my journal several times, then watching the events unfold in the news, I decided to turn those journal entries into a book.

I had never written a book before, but I felt that my concern about the upcoming election might very well come true. The book was meant to serve as a warning of what could occur if the president did not to accept the election results, attempt to circumvent the U.S. Constitution, and use any means to stay in power.

After the first book was published, a series of events, very similar to what had been written in the book began to unfold. The news coverage in the summer and fall of 2020 made me feel very uncomfortable. My concerns started to seemingly become reality.

The president indeed declared that the election was somehow rigged and refused to concede. He used conspiracy theories that were all disproven to back up his claims. His supporters no longer appeared to care about facts. They bought into his lies.

They had been sold a 21st century 'snake oil' that was meant to be the cure-all to what they believed to be their problems. His lies eventually led to the events that unfolded on January 6th, 2021. This is a date that should never be forgotten as it was an insurrection, an attempted coup, an assault on our democracy.

For those of you that read the first book, you will notice that it ended on that date. My fear then was that our nation would descend into a civil war on that day because of that president refusing to leave office and unconstitutionally hang onto power. What unfolded that day was an attempt to end democracy as we know it. Fortunately, for all of us, they failed.

What if they had not failed though? Where would we be as a nation and as a world if they succeeded? Would the citizens of this nation just stand by and let the nation fall to a tyrant? With the nation so divided, would there be a chance for reason and logic to prevail or would chaos and fealty to one person reign the future? Would we see the end of democracy in our lifetime? This book explores that possibility.

It starts on the same day as the first book ends but goes back in time earlier in that day to include a similar insurrection as what unfolded in real life. It carries the reader into an alternate reality where the insurrectionists, the emboldened president, and his accomplices have successfully circumvented democracy to keep the president in power.

When you read this book, ask yourself a few questions. Can this happen in the United States of America? Are we so comfortable with our democratic norms that we take democracy for granted so much that we do not see how easily it can be taken away from us? Is what we see unfolding in our current post-election society just a slow unraveling of democracy? Will we stand up against any threat to our democracy? Will you stand up for what is right, even if it leads to the ultimate sacrifice?

Thankfully, it turns out that my concerns did not occur quite the way I envisioned. However, the actions that did occur that day and in the days since should serve as a warning to all of us that democracy is not something we can take for granted. Our forebearers knew that what they embarked on as an experiment in democracy could easily fall to a tyrant. They created a government, that although imperfect, could have the greatest chance of survival and success for the people. It is our responsibility to ensure that this nation continues to stand.

"TYRANNY ARISES ON SOME FAVORABLE EMERGENCY."

— JAMES MADISON

CHAPTER 1

INSURRECTION

January 6th, 2021

T he day was expected to be quite eventful. A joint session of Congress is scheduled to meet to confirm the presidential electoral college outcome. Although there was much controversy surrounding the election, President Donald E. Vil had run a fairly successful post-election disinformation campaign that threw the entire 2020 presidential election into chaos. The false claims of Chinese election meddling, the constant attacks on the media, and the untimely death of his rival Joe Wilson, led enough electors to change their votes in favor of reelecting President Vil. The successful disinformation campaign resulted in overturning the will of the majority of American voters and the electoral outcome of the states the electors represent.

The 2020 election had the outcome of maintaining Republican control of the U.S. Senate, the change of power to the Republicans in the U.S. House, and once the certification of the electoral votes was complete, the reelection of President Vil. The Supreme Court was on the verge of a 7-2 conservative majority after President Vil nominated two loyalists the week prior, following the untimely deaths of the two most liberal leaning judges. President Vil was now the most powerful president in modern history. He would be able to accomplish every one of his goals and dismantle the very nation he oversaw from within. The consolidation of power entirely in his hands was almost complete.

In the morning, President Vil prepared for a rally that was scheduled to start at noon in front of the White House. He expected a large group of supporters to attend after several weeks of claiming election fraud. He wanted to create a day of controversy and put pressure on Congress to ensure they vote to validate the electoral outcome in his favor. He had not informed anyone involved in the rally of the content of his speech, but at the rally he planned to declare himself the most popular president in American history and demand that he be made president for life.

As the noon hour approached and the crowd rolled in, it became obvious that the turnout was larger than had been expected. His daughter, and now Vice President, Sophia Kaiser, preceded her father's speech. She claimed that her father was so popular that Congress should repeal the 22nd Amendment, in order for him to run for president again and implement his desire for his view of American greatness. As she concluded her speech, the president was informed that a large crowd had assembled at Capitol Hill to protest the electoral proceedings and his hijacking of democracy. This angered him greatly, as he believed that no one should challenge his power and his greatness. In that moment, he decided to make a minor change to his speech.

He rallied the crowd of almost a million spectators for over an hour, making false claims of voter fraud and election meddling. They ignored the social distancing from the ongoing worldwide pandemic. The crowd was energetic, visibly angry, and ready for confrontation. Vil sensed the energy of the crowd and unleashed his fury of hate!

"My fellow true patriots, it is time to let the rest of the American people know that this nation is now our nation! I am the chosen one to lead us to greatness!" he started.

The cheers from the crowd grew loud. He knew it was time to send them to do his bidding.

He continued, "Just before I started speaking to you, I learned that there is a gathering of rioters at the Capitol building. These violent people hate our country and do not want to see me remain as your president. They want to take away our right to run this nation as we see fit! I compel you to let your voices be heard! Let us march to the Capitol together and prevent them from stopping the certification of my win! The greatest victory in all of history!

"We can no longer let these evil anti-American losers have any say over our democracy. They want to take away our rights and give power to those that are not faithful to the nation like you. They want to destroy our nation so that China and other nations can have great power over us. They want to ruin our way of life. Now is the time for us to call on all true patriots to demand that I be instated as your president for life! Now go be good patriots and deliver my message and my wrath!"

With that, the large crowd marched toward the Capitol, to confront the protestors that Vil labeled as rioters. The air was heavy with anticipation as the crowd approached the Capitol building. The moment was ripe for violence.

SIEGE AT DEMOCRACY'S DOORSTEP

The new Speaker of the House of Representatives and Senate Majority Leader, Senator McDaniels, walked out of the Speaker's office after final discussions about the electoral vote confirmation that was about to commence. Both men were skeptical of the claims of election meddling and voter fraud by the president, but they were pleased to be in control of every seat of government. They had visions of what the future of the republic looked like with their hands on the levers.

However, they did not know what the president's plans were for the future of democracy. The Speaker gaveled in the joint session of Congress to ceremoniously confirm the electoral college vote and validate the reelection of President Vil to a second term. As they began the process of certifying the vote, a large gathering of protestors assembled outside the Capitol building. They chanted, "not our president," while holding signs that read: "Vil is a fraud," "stolen election," and "cheater," among many others. Their chants of outrage were not heard, as the chamber began to certify the electors for President Vil.

The protest continued into it's third hour as larger crowd of people began to emerge in the distance, along the Capitol Mall route. The Vil supporters were working their way to confront the protestors at the Capitol building. When Vil's supporters reached the Capitol, several of them began to brandish the weapons they had concealed. It appeared to the protestors that Vil's supporters had come armed with handguns, baseball bats, pepper spray, crowbars, and tasers.

What unleashed over the next several hours, began as a verbal assault, but quickly devolved into a brutal attack. Vil's supporters used their weapons to beat the protestors. Several were beaten so extensively, they needed immediate urgent care, which was nowhere to be found. The remaining anti-Vil protestors dispersed as quickly as they could from the violent mob of Vil supporters. Many could not escape in time and were fatally beaten by the mob. Capitol Hill police officers attempted to intervene and stop the violence. The size of the mob easily outnumbered the police force, forcing them to retreat to the footsteps of the Capitol building.

As the violent attack occurred outside the Capitol building, the joint session of Congress was temporarily halted by the Speaker of the House to ensure the safety of the legislators. For several hours the mob continued their assault outside the Capitol building. They unleashed a bloodbath on the doorsteps of the citadel of democracy.

When they found themselves with no more protestors left to assault, they turned their fury to the Capitol building itself, breaking anything they could get their hands on. When they finally broke into the Capitol building, they destroyed and defecating on statues, attempted to hunt down politicians, and continued their assault on the Capitol police. Their actions caused the eyes of the world to focus on them and question the viability of a future for American democracy. It was late into the evening before the National Guard was called in to disperse them. Everyone that was involved in the insurrection was able to flee without being arrested.

The president was watching the live coverage of the insurrection from his private quarters within the White House, as it evolved. He had grown excited to see his most faithful followers so loyal to him that they had attacked peaceful protestors and laid siege to the capitol building. He was rooting them on and hoping they would be able to obstruct the electoral college vote count in a final attempt to show the legislators that they cannot defy him. There was a knock at the door to his quarters, it was the head of his Secret Service detail.

"Enter!" shouted an anxious President Vil.

"Mr. President, I am here to inform you that the National Guard has been activated and they are enroute to the capitol to stop the violence."

"No! We must allow this to unfold so that we can create more chaos! The violence that is happening is just making a greater case for why I must be installed as the leader of this nation indefinitely!" Vil screamed back to the agent.

"I'm sorry Mr. President, there is nothing that I can do. There is just so much going on right now that we do not have any control over."

"Get out of here then so I can formulate a plan. I can still make this work in my favor."

The agent left the quarters, allowing President Vil space to think. Everything had been going as he wanted and now it was ending abruptly.

"How can I get this to shift back in my favor? If the momentum stays on my side, then I can get Congress to circumvent the Constitution and make me the president for the rest of my life!" he thought as he paced back and forth.

It came to him. He must immediately address the nation live on television. He can claim that his supporters went to the capitol to defend it from the violent protestors that wanted to stop him from being reelected. They only went into the building to ensure the safety of the legislators. Any violence that occurred had only been caused by the angry protestors and not his supporters. Yes, these were the events he would describe to the American people. Then, he would declare a national emergency and call on the Congress to subvert the Constitution and install him as the nation's leader indefinitely.

There was no time to waste. He called his secretary and informed her to have a camera ready to go live in fifteen minutes. He used the time to lay out his talking points and then wash up before going to the Oval Office. He was greeted by a few members of his staff that were anticipating what he would say during his address to the nation. He took his seat at the desk, looked into the camera and gave the cue to the cameraman.

"My fellow Americans, today our nation was attacked by a violent mob of anti-American protestors that refused to accept my impressive electoral victory. Thankfully, my loyal supporters stood up to this evil and prevented them from their attempt to destroy our way of life. We must not allow these acts to continue. Over the last several weeks, we have all seen the violence that has occurred from this anti-American movement.

"Now is the time to stop this evil before this cancer can metastasize. I want to see us restore our nation to the great place it once was before these anti-Americans came and took our jobs and destroyed our way of life! I am calling on all true patriots to stand up against this evil! We need your help to make America great again!

"Therefore, I am activating our entire U.S. Armed Forces, including the reserves. I am also asking every armed militia group to rally around our military and assist them in weeding out this evil from our nation. We need your help to restore our way of life! You will hear more about our plans in the coming days and weeks."

The president signaled to end the live broadcast to the nation. His short speech, if effective, was enough to deflect attention from what his mob of supporters had done only hours ago and put the blame back on anyone that opposed him. He knew his most fervent supporters would subscribe to his calls for action, but he hoped those on the sidelines would finally be swayed in his direction as well.

ATTEMPT TO SUBVERT DEMOCRACY

Hours had passed since the insurrection had been averted by National Guard troops. The Speaker of the House was ready to reconvene Congress and finish what they had started, to certify President Vil as the winner of the election. This certification would ignore the will of the people and usurp the legitimate outcome of the electoral process.

The joint session of Congress returned to the chamber to finish what they had begun hours earlier. Over the next few hours, senators and representatives of the Republican party praised Vil's leadership and calls for an end to the uprisings. In contrast, their Democrat party equivalents, attacked the unconstitutionality of the electoral vote and the legitimacy of Vil becoming a second-term president, at the defiance of the outcome of the election. They called on his declaration of war against China the day before, and his current calls for attacks against American citizens, as an act to solidify power in his hands.

They continued their ongoing debate over their constitutional responsibility. Meanwhile, as the nine o'clock evening hour approached, several members of Congress became distracted by alerts on their cell phones. Mumbling amongst the members began to grow into loud chatter. The Speaker of the House reached for his phone to see what the chatter was all about.

"California Governor to speak to the nation at any moment!" the alert read.

The chatter amongst the group prompted the Speaker of the House to attempt restoring order in the chamber. It was too late. Their eyes were glued to their phones as the coverage went live to California Governor Rosa Perez. She gave an impassioned speech about how the nation had fallen into the hands of a dictator with complicity from the legislative branch and a takeover of the judicial branch. She prompted Americans to stand up for their constitutional duty to protect the nation.

She called on Donald E. Vil to step aside as president and allow democracy to prevail. The chamber was eerily quiet during her speech. She concluded her remarks by asking for her fellow Americans to stand up against tyranny and be willing to fight to save American democracy. It was her belief that if the democratic process was averted in order to install someone that the majority party in Congress desired to be in power, then the entire democratic experiment would fail.

Their phone screens went blank after she concluded her remarks. The chamber erupted in boisterous applause by the Democrat members who hoped this was enough to stop the proceedings. The Republican members yelled back in defiance, calling it a 'takeover' and a 'coup'. Violence in the chamber was eminent.

Then, before any fists could be unleashed, the chamber went dark. The speaker was unaware of what was happening, but he feared the worst. As loud as his voice could muster, he yelled for everyone to evacuate the chamber.

Panic ensued as the congressional members stampeded their way out of the chamber. Not only had the power gone out in the Capitol building, but the nation's entire power grid had been shut down.

CHAPTER 2

NATION IN THE DARK

HEADQUARTERS OF THE RESISTANCE

January 6th, 2021

Conrad Augustus entered the new command center where the resistance movement had relocated their headquarters. Under the cloak of darkness, the resistance leadership team had fled Sacramento, California to their new command center hidden deep in the Sierra Nevada mountains. The secret location had been transformed from a former Cold War era bunker, long since abandoned, that only a handful of government officials knew still existed.

Conrad threw his medium-sized duffel bag on the bottom bed of the bunk where he was about to share a room with several members of the resistance for the foreseeable future. He was exhausted and ready for a few hours of rest following several weeks of non-stop planning. They had spent many sleepless nights preparing for what was about to unfold. This quickly prepared plan was a last-ditch effort to save the nation from the tyrannical president who was hell bent on refusing to leave office after his narrow re-election loss.

Conrad grabbed his toiletry bag and headed for the shared restroom to clean up before getting some rest. He wrapped his towel around his waist, put his bag down on the sink, grabbed his toothbrush and toothpaste. As he brushed his teeth, he could not help but stare at the man looking back at him. He felt like he no longer recognized himself.

His dark hair appeared to have grayed very quickly over the previous weeks. Deep wrinkles had emerged around his sharp blue eyes. He had even put on a few more pounds around his waist from working endless days that led into the night, preventing him from his daily workout regimen that he had continued even after his retirement from the Navy.

He thought about the preceding weeks and months that had led up to this point. The country had just experienced four years under a president that spent the entire term attacking anyone that disagreed with him. A president that used childish name-calling tactics to go after those that spoke out against his policies. He had used the office of the presidency to attack people based on their religious affiliation, heritage, politics, ethnicity, gender, and sexual identity. He had demanded absolute loyalty of his advisors. Not absolute loyalty to the nation, the Constitution, or the rule of law; but to him personally.

As the days closed in on the presidential election, President Donald E. Vil had grown more out of control. He spent all his time and energy attacking his opponent, smearing his good name with lies. He closed the borders with Canada and Mexico to send a message that he was in control and could punish our neighbors with the stroke of a pen. He ignored a raging global pandemic that had cost too many Americans their lives and their livelihoods. Almost half a million Americans had lost their lives from the pandemic, while the president ignored it so he could focus his energy and time on finding any way to stay in power at all costs.

After he lost his re-election bid to his political opponent, he went on television to state that the election was a fraud. He lied to the American people by claiming that his political opponent and the Chinese government conspired to manipulate the election to make President Vil lose the election. In fact, it was President Vil that had conspired with Russian President Vladimir Porchensky to interfere in the presidential election.

All of this was now known to Conrad and a small group within the resistance. The former Speaker of the House had passed along the intelligence report from within our own government that confirmed what many had long suspected; that the U.S. President had colluded with the Russians. When President Vil discovered that the Speaker of the House had been briefed on this material and passed it along, he had her arrested and charged with treason based on bogus allegations. She had in fact done the greatest thing she could have done; she gave the resistance the confirmation that President Vil was indeed a traitor to the republic.

The country was now in turmoil. Protests and riots had broken out all over the nation. Many protests were in support of President Vil, while just as many protests demanded for his resignation. Citizens were fearful every day of the possibility of civil war after President Vil had unconstitutionally hung onto power. He was now only a few days from being sworn in for a second term. What complicated the matter was that it was not so much that the people feared a pending civil war, it is that they knew it was inevitable, while many citizens even embraced it!

Conrad finished brushing his teeth and placed his belongings back in his bag. He took another long look in the mirror, wondering if he would end up dying as a traitor or as someone involved in saving the republic. The future was unknown, but no matter the outcome he was not willing to stand on the sidelines. He had made his choice and would now have to answer for it. He pressed play on his small portable out of date iPod. It was the only technological device he could bring with him on this journey due to electronic surveillance concerns. He stepped into the shower as the light jazz played in the background, allowing him to relax just a little.

URGENT MESSAGE

"Hello, Mr. Conrad. I'm sorry to bother you but the Governor has requested to speak with you immediately," came the voice of a young man in an awkward looking military-style uniform.

Startled out of his deep sleep, Conrad looked at his watch. It was 1:35 in the morning. It was now January 7th, 2021. He had only slept for a few hours. He looked up at the soldier, unable to recognize him from the group he had been working with for the last few weeks.

"What's going on? Why can this not wait? And what is that uniform you are wearing?" he asked.

The young soldier replied, "They didn't tell me, sir. I am just a lonely private for the resistance. This is actually my father's old uniform from when he served in the army. It is quite outdated. They told me that we cannot wear the same uniforms as the enemy or else we could easily get confused and mistaken for them."

"Well young man, they are not our enemy. They are our brothers and sisters. They are the opposition," he paused a moment to think. "Many of them are just confused and believe that they are meant to be loyal to the president and his orders. They may not fully understand or appreciate their oath. They are supposed to be loyal to the Constitution. If a president breaks their oath or commits an act of treason or refuses to accept our democratic process, then they must do what is right, like you did, and fight for the republic. If they join our ranks like you did, then they will be on the right side of history."

"I understand what you are saying. I definitely should not consider our fellow soldiers and citizens the enemy. We just don't agree on how our democratic process was attacked and how we became so polarized that we got to this point. I hope that whatever happens over these coming days and weeks will set us on the right path to reunite as one nation again."

"E pluribus unum," Conrad stated.

"I'm sorry?" the young soldier asked.

"Out of many, one. It is our nation's motto. We are a people that have come from all walks of life, we all have our own traditions, beliefs, religions, ethnicity, cultural differences, etc.; but we fundamentally are one united people. Not everyone fully embraces that philosophy, but if we are to remain united as a nation and emerge out of this dark period in our history, then we must remember our motto and these simple words, 'united we stand, divided we fall.'"

"Well, Mr. Conrad, now I know why the general calls you the teacher. You must have a lot of knowledge about our history."

Conrad chuckled.

"I suppose I have some. I was a high school civics teacher before this. And please, call me Conrad, drop the Mr., I'm your brother, not your boss. And what is your name?"

"My name is Michael. Nice meeting you Conrad. I wish you had been my civics teacher. I never really enjoyed that class in school. My teacher never really connected with our class and did not make it particularly interesting."

"I am sorry that you had that experience Michael. I will tell you what though, you are being an active participant in our civics by joining the resistance to save our democracy. It seems to me that you did take something out of that class."

"Geez, I guess I never thought about it like that."

"Tell me Michael, how did you end up joining so quickly? I know that we are currently in the process of dropping leaflets to spread the word, but how did you get to be here with us in the Sierra Nevada and so close to the leadership team as a private?"

"That is an interesting story. I was serving as an infantryman in the army when the election happened. I was stationed at Ft. Hood. When the president declared that the election was a fraud and he would not leave office, I knew something was wrong. I have never been one to care much about politics, but I do believe that this nation has a fundamental obligation to uphold democracy. Our commander told us that we were to prepare for possible violence and to squash any uprisings. I knew this was wrong, we are not allowed to use the military against our own citizens. After that day I took off my uniform, left and never went back."

"That is a very brave move to take knowing that you could be charged with going AWOL."

"I know, but the alternative was to do something that I know goes against our core values. My father would be ashamed had I not left."

"Your father must be proud of you for standing up for democracy?"

"I hope so. He actually died last year at the beginning of the pandemic after he contracted the virus. I joined the army last summer, after he died, to make him proud."

"I am sorry to hear about your father. I believe he is proud of you for what you are doing. You are about to embark on something that, if we win the hearts and minds of the people, will unite us to ensure that our democracy survives."

"Thank you for that Conrad."

"So, you never explained how you got here."

"Oh, yes, about that. I had found my way out to Las Vegas where my aunt lives, and the army could not track me down. I was watching the riots on television a few weeks ago and something inside me told me that I had to more than just walk away from the army; I had to do more. The next day I drove to San Francisco and found some people that were protesting and joined with them. I guess I made a strong impression because that night I was introduced to a woman that told me that if I wanted to do more than protest, I could join some of them leaving the next morning. She said it was an underground resistance movement. That brought me here to the mountains. To be honest, I don't even know exactly where we are, we have not had our phones with us since we left San Francisco. We had to wear a head covering the entire way here."

"Well, Michael, you have made that right decision. You are a brave young man, and your heart is guiding you well. I look forward to working with you."

"Thank you. I just want my father to be proud of me," Michael stated while looking up at the ceiling as if he were looking at heaven.

"I know your father is proud of you," Conrad paused momentarily, "I had a student this last school year that shares the Spanish version of your name, his name is Miguel. You remind me of him. He is too young to be involved in what we are doing, but he too worried about what was happening before the election and since then. I hope he and his mother are safe," he paused again, thinking about how he had left so abruptly from teaching to do what he had now embarked on. "Well, why don't you take me to the governor now. We have kept her waiting long enough."

"Oh yes, we must hurry, she sounded urgent about speaking with you."

Michael quickly turned around, gesturing for Conrad to follow, heading down the corridor enroute to the main briefing room. When they arrived, the young soldier let Conrad pass to go inside. Governor Perez was waiting patiently. Conrad thanked the soldier and entered the room. The young soldier closed the door behind Conrad and stood guard in front of the door.

A MESSAGE OF HOPE

"Conrad, thank goodness you are here. I was beginning to wonder if you were okay," exclaimed a now relieved Governor Perez.

"Please forgive my delay, I was just talking with a young soldier. Is everything alright?" Conrad asked.

"Well, no…I mean yes. Look, at the screens. Most of the nation is in the dark after our successful shut down of the nation's three separate power grids. Thanks to our preplanning we were able to position our assets in places to track the response to our message about the coming turmoil our nation is about to experience. Look at the drone footage," she stated, gesturing her hand for Conrad to look out the window of her office to the command center below, where several screens displayed drone footage of several cities around the nation.

"It looks like people are leaving the cities."

"Yes, that's exactly what is happening. It appears our message might be working. With all the unrest going on in the nation, my address to the nation, our shutdown of the power grids, and the leaflets that have been dropped in several cities tonight, our message might very well be resonating with patriotic Americans. Our message will continue to spread with many more leaflets being dropped from planes over the coming days.

"Americans are getting the picture and they are going to the locations that the leaflets have designated as their closest resistance outposts. So far we are assessing that almost a million Americans are leaving the cities and heading to our outposts."

"But are they all going to the locations we have designated as resistance outposts or are some of these people just fleeing the cities to avoid getting involved?

"We won't be assured of that for several days, once we have been able to get our message to the majority of Americans. Conrad, what I'm more afraid of at this point is people penetrating our numbers that are not loyal to the nation, but ready to infiltrate our numbers for Vil."

"I see that as a possibility. His faithful followers are very radical and have shown that they are willing to do almost anything. What do the generals say about that?"

"They urge caution and have recommended that we should conduct polygraph tests on everyone that joins our numbers."

"That's impossible! We are talking about hundreds of thousands if not millions of Americans that would have to be polygraphed. There is just no feasible way to do that."

"I know, but there is really no other way that we can assure we do not have spies join our ranks."

"Governor, there will never be a one hundred percent way to prevent spies from joining our ranks. If you want my recommendation, I believe we spend the limited resources of polygraphing to those that we entrust within leadership. There might be some spies that penetrate our military ranks and they may very well be able to take out some of our forces, but our casualties will be limited. I know that isn't the best alternative, but it will be nearly impossible to do what the generals are recommending."

"Thank you, Conrad, I knew you could offer a fresh perspective. Unfortunately, you are right. We do have very limited resources and we will end up having spies infiltrate our ranks. Thank you for your advice."

"Of course! We have to maximize our limited resources and capabilities and focus those efforts on our main goal. To win the republic back for the sake of democracy," Conrad replied.

"That reminds me, you have not heard about Vil's speech tonight. Given that we were in a total communications blackout while we prepared for and delivered the speech last night, I have some very heavy news to break to you. Yesterday, while Congress was unconstitutionally certifying the election results, a mob of Vil supporters laid siege to the U.S. Capitol. They attacked anti-Vil protestors outside the capitol and then turned toward the capitol itself. They broke in and destroyed as much as they could before they were finally forced out by national guard troops."

"How did this happen?" Conrad asked.

"Vil himself, incited them with a fiery speech attacking our very democracy. He urged them to go to the capitol and take whatever action necessary to ensure he remained in power."

"And they just did what he commanded?"

"Yes! That is what worries me about their willingness to fight for this man. Most of his followers will stop at nothing to do his bidding."

"Then we have a greater challenge ahead of us than we originally anticipated. We will need to really focus on promoting the message that democracy itself is at stake so that we can urge more Americans to get involved."

"We have a heavy taken on a heavy burden and have a very complicated task ahead of us. Get some rest, the morning will be here soon, and we have a long day ahead of us tomorrow."

"Goodnight, Governor," Conrad said as he turned to leave. He stopped before stepping out of the room. "Governor, given the recent development, may I offer a recommendation?"

"I have a feeling that you will offer it no matter my reply."

A lop-sided smile appeared across Conrad's face. "I think you need a new title, one that matches your position as the leader of the resistance. I do not think that the title of Governor is one commensurate with your role. There are several governors that are involved with our movement to restore democracy. If you want to ensure our forces follow your lead, then you should have a title that commands the respect of what we are doing."

"It is just a title, I do not see it as anything more or less than just that."

"Then why even have a title at all? Some people may use this opportunity of crisis to make a power grab and take authority and control from you. That will most likely happen if something does not go in our favor. And we know that is bound to happen at some point; probably sooner rather than later."

"Conrad, I will spend some time to consider your recommendation. Now go get some rest. We have a long day tomorrow and it will begin very soon."

"Goodnight, Governor Perez."

Conrad walked out of the office, leaving the Governor to think about his recommendation. He hoped he would knock out the moment his head rested on his pillow to get a few more hours of rest before the long day ahead.

THE RESISTANCE TO TYRANNY

January 7th, 2021

The morning arrived quickly for Conrad. His alarm sounded promptly at 6 a.m. He popped out of his bunk as if he had not just been awake a few hours prior. The former Navy chief petty officer in him sprang to life. He did a quick set of pushups to get his heart rate up so he could feel awake and ready to tackle the long day ahead. He then showered and put on a gray two-piece ensemble that roughly resembled a military uniform.

Conrad had not worn a uniform in several years. He felt quite uncomfortable looking at his reflection in the mirror. He had reluctantly accepted that with his role in leadership he would need to be recognizable in front of whatever armed forces they would soon assemble. The feeling of being so close to the upper echelons of the resistance made Conrad feel quite out of his element. He turned and left for the main conference room for their first morning briefing.

When Conrad arrived, he was greeted by several other senior members of the newly formed resistance forces. He recognized several political elites that had left their positions in government, some retired generals and admirals, and many of the same CEO's and business leaders that had joined them only weeks prior. They were all committed to the same goal: to quickly remove the unconstitutionally re-elected President Vil from the presidency and restore democracy to the nation.

Conrad made some small talk with one of the politicians from his home state of Iowa. He had come out to the bunker to receive guidance on how to form a local resistance force and band together with the much more established forces on the coasts and other major metropolitan cities. While they were discussing the current situation in a much less recognizable Iowa than Conrad grew up in, a silence grew over the assembled group as they noticed Governor Perez enter. She stepped to the podium while everyone took the seats available, leaving many to stand next to the walls.

"Good morning, everyone," she began. "It is good to see everyone's faces this morning. I recognize several of you as we have worked together over the last few years. I also see some of you that have joined our resistance over the last few weeks. For those of you that I have not yet met, let me thank you now for your patriotism and mutual interest to save our republic and restore the constitutionality of our government. We have a daunting task ahead, so let us not spend too much time on formalities.

"As you know, last night we shut down the nation's power grids. This was not an easy task since the grid is not connected throughout the nation. Our team hacked each of the three grids and secured a nationwide shut down after I addressed the nation last night. While this has secured us the freedom to move about without the worry of being tracked through electronic means, and this does buy us some time, we still have some outstanding issues that need to be addressed.

"I have been informed that the shutdown will only guarantee us a few days advantage before authorities are able to uncover the virus placed in their electronic systems that took the power grids down. Once these systems are able to be brought back online, my team will be able to continue to attack the grids, but with less effective results. Altogether, we are looking at up to a week of almost entire darkness followed by up to a month of intermittent power outages.

"Additionally, we have been able to take the nations satellite systems and missiles systems offline for now. Most of the country's military bases have emergency power grids, so we cannot guarantee they have all gone dark. However, we do assess several bases," pointing to a map on the wall with several bases annotated for their lack of long-term power supply, "will have a limited back up power supply. We will need to take advantage of that in the coming days.

"Our experts are working hard to maintain total satellite darkness for as long as we possibly can. We will need to communicate through shortwave radio and messengers. I know, it's very 'old school' but the only way that we have an advantage right now is by placing Vil's forces back into the dark ages for as long as we can. Once we lose the advantage we have given ourselves, we will have a long, dark and uncertain future ahead of us. We must quickly assemble anyone that is willing to stand up for this great nation, give them weapons, provide them military leadership, and strike fast. We have only days before we lose the advantage we have right now.

"What you may not know already is that an insurrection on the U.S. Capitol occurred yesterday. While Congress was attempting to certify the election results, Vil held a rally for thousands of his supporters. He urged them to march to the U.S. Capitol and attack protestors assembled outside that were demanding he leave office. They did his bidding and attacked the protestors, then turned their sights on the capitol where they broke in and caused major destruction. National guard troops were finally called in. This attack on our capitol might put momentum on our side to ensure a swift return to democracy.

"If you will now excuse me, I am leaving with some of my military commanders to go to Los Angeles to address whoever is there and ready to join our ranks. I will leave you in the hands of the leader of our resistance forces, General Isaac Hamilton, and the chief of our information warfare operations team, Brigadier General Conrad Augustus. May you all be guided by the belief that our strength comes from our unity."

Governor Perez stepped away from the podium and departed the room. She left many questions unanswered for the group. General Hamilton stepped up to the podium to speak. Conrad developed confused look on his face when he learned he had just been given such a senior military role. He had not expected the governor to give him a formal military title, although he had been an important advisor. Even she had still not adopted a formal title, something he believed would give her more authority in the long term.

General Hamilton and Conrad briefed the group for the next hour about the first strike plan that they called Operation Fire Storm. They answered the many questions that were posed of them. They were also asked about the potential for success for the operation. They had to admit to everyone that the plan was not a guarantee and that it required several complicated elements to align. However, it was the best available option they had against the strength, experience, and awesome power of the U.S. Armed Forces.

DEVOTION TO FREEDOM

Governor Perez arrived in Los Angeles just after noon. She was transported by several different means to ensure that she would not be tracked. When she arrived at Los Angeles, they took a helicopter to their final destination. She was accompanied by a small security detail and some advisors. She was uncertain of what to expect but hopeful that she had been received as a leader of the resistance.

Her voice was not the first to declare the illegitimacy of Donald Vil as president, but she was the most influential. She was the only leader that could convince the resistance factions, rioters, looters, and the many citizens that felt disinterested, to join forces to stand up for freedom and the constitution. She hoped that her message the night before had resonated with enough Americans that they could mobilize a force strong enough and fast enough that could overwhelm the forces they would encounter. If their plan did not materialize in the way they anticipated, she feared countless deaths and even the collapse of democracy forever.

The helicopter pilot gestured to the governor as they neared their destination. She looked below at a large crowd assembled at the top of the hill at Griffith Observatory. She has selected the location because as a child her parents took her to the observatory. She fell in love with the view of the bustling city below and the stars in the sky above that could only be seen at night if the smog had dissipated.

The pilot landed the helicopter and a member of her security detail escorted her to the podium so she could address the audience. She felt an awkward heat emanating from the sun considering the winter season. She gestured to a member of her detail, who then spoke into an encrypted radio. Within seconds the sound of the power grid came rolling to life. Those in attendance noticed their cell phone signals reactivate. The green light activated on the camera that had been positioned to capture the event.

"Good afternoon, my fellow Americans. Let me start by introducing myself once again. My name is Rosa Perez, I am the leader of the resistance movement. We are a group of proud Americans that have watched the quick collapse of democracy over the last few weeks. We are here to protect our nation from falling into the hands of a dictator.

"I can confirm to you that Donald E. Vil has refused to step aside and allow the American democratic process to continue. He believes that he is entitled to rule over us for a generation. He has installed his own daughter as his apprentice so that she can one day succeed him. This is not part of our democratic process. This is not American.

"We as Americans must make the decision today whether we will stand on the right side of history…," pausing for a moment as she rethought her words, then she continued, "the right side of our 'human story,' or whether we will allow democracy to fail, our nation to fall, and the world to succumb to chaos.

"This is our time to do what is right no matter how much it will disrupt our daily lives. If we do not step up to this moment, then we will fall to tyranny. At my direction, the nation went dark last night. The nation will once again go dark at the conclusion of my remarks. Donald E. Vil will not leave peacefully, therefore we must unite and remove him and his allies from power so that we can restore democracy and unite our nation so that we can heal and move forward.

"Let this be a warning that if you do not stand with us, you stand against us. We will restore our nation to the republic for which it stands. Last night we began to drop leaflets that explains how to join the resistance and where the nearest camp is located from your city. These leaflets have been dropped in several cities and we will continue to have them distributed over the coming days to smaller cities and towns as well as rural communities.

"I urge you to join us on the right side of our human story. Let us unite and save our nation…for the sake of our children. The fate of the nation now rests in your hands."

She stepped away from the podium. As she returned to the helicopter, her attention was directed toward a little girl at the front of the crowd waving at her next to a man she assumed was her father. A feeling inside her forced her to turn from her path and approach the girl.

She noticed the little girl was not more than eight years old. She had dark brown hair and bold brown eyes. When the girl noticed that the governor was approaching her direction, she looked up at her father not knowing what she should do if the governor stopped in front of them. Her father just smiled and pointed his finger in the direction of the governor, so that his daughter would turn her eyes to notice that she was indeed stopping to confront them.

The governor stopped in front of the girl, leaned down on one leg, and asked, "Hello young lady, may I ask your name?"

The girl replied, "My name is Maya. This is my father, Jose."

"Maya, it is nice to meet you and your father. Can I ask what brought you out here today?"

"My father brought me here. He said that we are going through some rough times right now and you might be able to make things better. Are you going to be able to make things safe for us?"

"Yes, you father is right. We are living in some very uncertain times. It is going to take every patriotic American to make the choice to stand up for what is right. But we will get through this, I have faith, and so should you."

"My father said he is going to send me to stay with my grandmother so that he can help you. I don't want him to go."

The governor looked up at the father. She recognized the look of worry on his face. She did not know this man, but she knew that whatever his troubles, he was willing to send his daughter to stay with her grandmother so that he could do what he felt to be his patriotic duty. This decision could not have been an easy one for him. In fact, it was not an easy decision for anyone to stand against your fellow citizen to stand for what you believe to be righteous.

"Well Maya, you should be proud of your father. He only wants what is best for you and he is willing to fight to give you a better future. Your father is a good man, I'm sure you already knew that." She looked up at the father and continued, "Thank you for what you are about to do. Our nation needs you. Our nation needs all of us to defend her."

"Thank you, ma'am. I just want to do my part," the father responded.

A member of the governor's security detail approached her and whispered in her ear to urge her to leave now for the helicopter.

"Well Maya, it was a pleasure to meet you. I must go now. I look forward to seeing you again one day soon when this is all over."

"Miss…what should we call you?" asked the father.

"You can call me Rosa."

"No, I mean what should we call you? In our church we call the man that leads the service our priest, at work I have a boss. You are leading this movement. What should we call you?"

"That is a great question sir. I suppose you can call me the Protectorate of American democracy," Rosa answered.

She looked back at young Maya, remembering her long ago youthful innocence. She felt as if it had been such a long time ago that she could barely remember her own childhood anymore. She thanked Maya's father for his willingness to join the resistance, got in helicopter bound for the bunker in the Sierra Nevada.

Although reluctant to take on a title of significance, she felt confident in her quick, on the spot decision. Governor Perez would now be known as Protectorate Perez, the leader of the resistance.

THE RESISTANCE GROWS

Conrad was using his satellite phone to finalize some last stages of Operation Fire Storm with his younger brother Atticus when the lights flickered. The power shut off and their call dropped. The generators kicked on and the power resumed, but only locally in the bunker. Conrad knew that the governor must have concluded her remarks and would be heading back soon. Their plan to restore power for a short time to get another message out to the citizens before shutting it all down again, he hoped had been a success.

Unfortunately for Conrad, that meant that he would not be able to give the final instructions and last-minute changes to his brother. Although they still had power in the bunker, the entire power grid was back off, leaving only businesses and homes with backup generators not in the dark. Cell phone towers and even their secure satellite phones would not function in this power outage. He had to trust that his brother Atticus would make the right decisions and go with his gut instinct.

He returned inside the bunker to see if there was still a growing response to their message over the last eighteen hours. Whatever action they intended to take would not be successful without the resounding support of the American people joining the resistance movement. He was pleasantly surprised as he monitored the screens that showed drone footage from several major cities. It appeared that there were significant numbers of people that were flocking to where their leaflets had directed them to go.

Conrad assessed that there were well over a million people that had already assembled throughout the nation with countless more flocking to these locations. Although pleased to see so many Americans ready to stand with them, this was not anywhere near the numbers they would need to stand up against Vil. Conrad hoped that it was still just too soon for most people to decide. They needed something compelling for them to be willing to fight with them instead of staying neutral. He was hopeful that in the coming days and weeks, their next actions would sway the undecided.

PREPARATION BEGINS

Rosa arrived back at the bunker late in the evening. She had expected to find the operations center almost empty, with only a small contingent working the night shift. However, she was greeted with a bustling team hard at work. She was not sure why everyone was still up and working so late into the night, but once she looked at the screens, she realized what the commotion was all about.

Several screens showed drown footage of fights taking place between citizens that had arrived at several of their locations. Some had signs to show their support for either the resistance or Vil, while others were carrying personal weapons such as baseball bats, batons, knives, and guns. While this was the scene in some locations, she saw a greater turnout in some locations and fewer in others, with no clashes between groups.

"General Hamilton, what is happening? We have to move quickly; time is of the essence here. Have we not dispatched our teams to these locations?" she asked.

"Ma'am, we sent our teams several hours ago, but without being able to communicate with them directly we are not sure where some of them are currently located. As you can see, several of our teams have arrived to greet our fellow citizens and inform them of their next steps. We assess that about three-fourths of our teams have arrived at their locations. We expect the remaining groups to make it to the areas where you see clashes happening within the next few hours."

"Why are they fighting?" she asked. "We are all on the same side."

"I'm afraid your concern about an infiltration by Vil supporters has happened. Once our teams arrive, we will be able to detain any hostiles and relocate them to facilities where they can be monitored."

"Good, let's get this plan into action. We have only a few days to get this right."

"When do the shipments of military weapons and supplies arrive or has China already betrayed us?" asked General Hamilton.

Conrad, who had been silently monitoring the screens, was caught off guard by what he had just heard. Had his ears betrayed him? Did General Hamilton just mention shipments of weapons from China? He did not remember this being part of the operation. His confused facial expression had now been noticed by Protectorate Perez.

"General Hamilton, Brigadier General Augustus, my office, please," she ordered.

Conrad was the last one to enter the office. He closed the door behind him for what he only suspected would be a deeply confidential conversation. If what he heard was true, then the entire operation was about to get very controversial for their cause.

"General, I was informed by our liaison in China that the six container ships of military vehicles, weapons, and equipment will arrive over the next few days. Three ships are expected to arrive in the Port of Long Beach by tomorrow, one in the San Francisco Bay and two in Seattle within three days time."

"That's good, we are going to need them off those ships as soon as they arrive. We have no time to spare. I've never trusted the Chinese; they better not hang us out to dry."

"General, I understand your concern, but we have made arrangements with them that benefits both sides."

"Very well, I need to get back on the floor. Oh, I am going to Las Vegas tomorrow. There is a casino tycoon out there that is willing to help fund our fight. He has billions of dollars to give and he knows several other billionaires that are patriotic and want to help us restore the nation. His only condition for now is that he wants to speak with me personally."

"Just make sure that you take your security detail, general. We cannot risk anything happening to you."

"Very well, goodnight, Governor."

"I have decided that I will go by Protectorate Perez from now on."

"I'm sorry, ma'am?" the general asked.

Looking over at Conrad, she responded, "Apparently I need a title, one that holds up to the moment. I was not elected to fill this role and therefore the title of governor no longer suits me. A Protectorate is someone charged with protecting and overseeing a state or territory. Since I was charged with protecting our American democracy, then it seems like a suitable title. Although, I would prefer that you refer to me as Rosa within our core leadership team. I have never been someone that liked formal titles."

"Very well, Rosa. I will update you on the status of our teams tomorrow before I leave for Las Vegas."

Once the general departed, Conrad immediately broke into a tirade.

"What are we doing working with China? I cannot believe I didn't know about this. So are they supplying us with arms?"

"Yes, Conrad, they are. I'm sorry I never mentioned this to you. I wanted to keep this information close hold for now. Both of our countries stand to gain by working together. They can provide us with the arms and munition to fight Vil to remove him from power, and we can lift the tariffs that Vil placed on them once we restore the nation."

"Still, I do not trust China. We need to be careful how we proceed with them. I want to be brought into the loop with all further negotiations with them."

"Understood Conrad. Look, we are going up against the greatest military in the world; our very own. We had to partner with someone, and they are the only country willing to assist us right now. I don't like it either, but sometimes you have to make a deal with the devil in order to have a fair fight."

CHAPTER 3

PRESIDENT IN CHAOS

THE WHITE HOUSE

January 6th, 2021

T
he Secret Service agents quickly rushed into the private residence of the White House within seconds of the power going out. It has only been moments since Governor Rosa Perez had concluded her address to the nation when the power went out. Moments later the emergency generators kicked on and the power resumed in the White House. The agents found a confused and bewildered President Donald Evan Vil sitting on the couch staring at a blank television.

The five agents grabbed the president and rushed him out of the residence. They surrounded him as they swiftly hurried him down to the main level of the White House, over to the East Wing and then down another flight of stairs into a basement. The lead Secret Service agent lifted his badge as they approached two agents guarding an armored door. The agent began yelling for them to swipe their badge and open the armored door so they could secure the president inside the Presidential Emergency Operations Center (PEOC).

The agent at the door swiped his badge and entered his code. The door sprung open and the agents pushed the president into the PEOC, three of them following him inside, while the rest remained outside to guard the door. Two agents searched the PEOC while the third remained with the president. After they secured the room, the third agent holstered his gun and gave the president the 'all clear.'

President Vil was out of breath. He took a seat at the conference table in front of him to rest and give his lungs a chance to regain their normal flow of oxygen. He remained baffled as to what had just happened. Was the nation under attack? Had the governor just declared war on him? This was his nation after all and a call to reject him as the rightful president was a call to war against him.

"Okay Mr. President, we are going to keep you here in the PEOC for a little longer, but it appears that we have no direct threat to you," the lead agent stated.

"What happened? I was watching my favorite cable news show on the Faux News Channel when the feed went blank. Then that crazy liberal governor from California came on the television to announce that she did not recognize me as the legitimate president and was declaring war against the United States."

"I don't know what is going on Mr. President. The word to 'secure mogul' came across my earpiece, which is our code to bring you to the bunker."

"So how long do I have to stay down here? I want to know what is going on! Someone tell me what is going on!"

The agent pressed his finger to his earpiece to drown out the complaining president. After a few seconds the agent replied, "Roger that, I will inform Mogul."

"Who is that? What is happening?"

"It appears that the nation's power grids have been hacked. The nation has gone dark."

"This is treason! It must be one of the militia groups. Maybe they are working together with that wretched governor from liberal California. I want her arrested!"

"Mr. President, your national security advisor is on his way. He should be here in less than five minutes. He will have an update for you."

SEDITION

President Vil waited nervously in the PEOC for his national security advisor to arrive. While waiting, he paced back and forth feeling as if something was not right. He believed he needed to get out of the PEOC and show some sort of leadership. He decided that once he spoke with his national security advisor, he would leave the PEOC. That is when the senior Secret Service agent pressed his earpiece against his ear again to get another update.

"Mr. President, your wife and youngest son were evacuated from the White House through the tunnels and taken to the Pentagon. They have arrived safely and are being taken below ground. Also, your national security advisor is here. If you could please stand back while we have the door opened."

President Vil realized he had completely forgotten about his wife and son. In order to appear as if he was concerned, replied, "Yes, that's good to hear that they are safe now. Now please let Bill Peterson in!"

The president stepped away from the door as the agent relayed through his lapel microphone for the door to be opened. All three agents had their guns aimed directly at Bill Peterson, the national security advisor, as he stepped inside. He had already been patted down but as soon as he entered the PEOC he was subjected to another security check. The only thing he brought with him was a bag full of files.

"It's about time you made it here Bill. What is going on? Why did we lose power?"

"Well Mr. President I was about to go home for the night when the California governor addressed the nation. I have some updates for you, but I will warn you that everything we know is preliminary and cannot be confirmed.

"What I can confirm is that several of the militia groups that we have been monitoring have been coordinating with each other to encourage the rioters and looters to disrupt our nation following your re-election. We have been tracking some major financial transactions over the last few weeks and believe that some very wealthy business owners might be funding some of these attacks. We also have reason to believe that China is pouring money into these efforts to cause chaos and destroy our nation.

"We are still conducting investigations into these transactions, but once we confirm these transactions, we can charge these individuals with committing major financial crimes and contributing to acts of sedition. Then we can seize their assets and stop the flow of money to these traitors."

"They are attempting a coup?"

"It appears as if that is their intent. From what we have been able to ascertain through our sources, they do not view you as the legitimate president. They plan to cause as much violence as possible until your supporters turn on you."

"Do they not get it? My supporters are with me until the end! I have given them a reason to back me no matter what. I built their wall to keep the Mexicans out, I caused a culture war between them and the elites, I dismantled everything my predecessor accomplished, I had that nasty Speaker of the House arrested on charges of treason, and I gave them a 7-2 conservative Supreme Court.

"I guess now it is time to arrest every Democrat member of Congress and have them questioned and charged with treason. Then I can have the remaining Republican members vote to repeal the 22nd Amendment. Then we can begin the process of me governing over this nation forever."

"Well Mr. President, I don't want to get into the politics of this, I am just here to ensure the safety of the homeland. I will do whatever you need me to do."

"Oh Bill, you just keep doing what I tell you and there will be a great reward for you one day. I want you to work with the Homeland Security Secretary to direct federal agents to have every Democrat party member of Congress arrested on charges of treason and sedition."

"We cannot confirm that any member of Congress is involved with this."

"Look Bill, I want them arrested. Charge them with terrorism for all I care. I just want them out of the picture so I can move forward with my plans."

"I suppose if we charge them with acts of terrorism then we can hold them indefinitely without actually informing any legal authorities. In fact, we can have them all transported to one of our interrogation facilities outside of the country."

"Yes! Yes! Do that! Now what does the governor of California have to do with this? Is she in on this as well? If so, I want her brought to me!"

"We do not actually have any information on what is going on out West. We are in the dark as of now."

"But just the other day, you updated me on a conspiracy to overthrow me and the intelligence reports you received showed that there were governors involved in this operation. They are all colluding against me! I want them all taken out!"

"Mr. President, it's not that easy. We have no direct evidence confirming that Governor Perez is involved in an attempted coup. Her statement tonight did not specifically call for you to be overthrown. She did call for citizens to do what she believes to be the right thing. However, she did not specifically call for a coup. Even if she does call for you to be overthrown, we have to look at the legal issues before we just go into a state to have a governor arrested. She has her own security detail, and a confrontation could get very ugly between state and federal authorities."

"I don't care what you have to do Bill, just make it happen! I need to show leadership and appear in control. If they take further action against me, it will make me look unprepared."

"Right away Mr. President. I will see what can be done. Do not get your hopes up just yet, this is a very delicate situation. We will have a much easier time rounding up the Democrat members of Congress."

The national security advisor departed the PEOC in a hurry, mulling over what legal options they could take against sitting governors to squash any potential coup.

President Vil took a seat at the conference table and reached for the phone in front of him.

"Someone get me President Porchensky on the phone."

THE RUSSIAN-AMERICAN ALLIANCE

President Vil continued to grow angry while waiting for a call back to connect him with Russian President Vladimir Porchensky. The assumption was that these were small factions of groups that were not highly coordinated and would not be able to pull off something of the size and scope of what just happened. He felt compelled to show strength and crush these factions.

As he sat behind his desk, he thought, "Who are they? How many people are involved in this coup attempt? Do they have someone on the inside helping them? Are they really willing to go up against the strongest military force in the world?" He knew he could get guidance from his mentor and friend Vladimir Porchensky. When the phone suddenly rang, he immediately felt a sense of relief come over him.

Vil picked up the phone and in a desperate voice asked, "Hello. Is this Vladimir? I need answers about what has happened!"

"No, Mr. President, this is the switchboard operator. I have President Porchensky on the line. I will connect you now."

"Hello, Dominik! How are you? Why are you calling me so early?" asked President Porchensky, using Donald Vil's Russian birth name to remind him of his loyalty to Russia and not the United States.

"Vladimir, it seems as though we have a problem. The militia groups that have not accepted the results of the election and my rightful claim to remain in power have taken out our nations power grids. We are completely in the dark. I think we underestimated them."

"No Dominik, you underestimated them. I knew exactly what you were dealing with. Our intelligence sources have been keeping me informed of that mess you have made over there."

"Well, why haven't you passed that information along to me so I could have prevented this attack?"

"Why would I do that my Dominik? Why would I let you spoil my fun? If you would have prevented this from occurring, then the U.S. might return to stability. We want this chaos to continue. This is what we hoped would result."

"But what if they attempt to assassinate me?" Vil asked.

"They won't be able to get close to you. You have the Secret Service guarding you. Plus, we have several of our own agents keeping guard over you. Look it's time that we begin the next phase of this operation."

"What is the next phase Vladimir? I thought the entire plan was to keep me in power. Is there something more?"

"It is time for you to unleash hell on America! Now is the time for you to declare that anyone who stands against you as a traitor and have them arrested. It's time for you to bring this nation under your full control! Display some ruthless leadership!"

"I will need a large military force for something like that. It might be time to begin a military draft."

"Yes, but make sure that you don't move too fast with any operation. Draw this out and make it last months or possibly years. It's time to really drain the United States and bring her to her economic and societal collapse!"

"What if my followers aren't ready for that? I am not sure that they are willing to go over that cliff yet. I have brought them along with me this far but destroying the nation this early in this game might backfire."

"You have rioters and looters in the streets. You have active militias plotting a coup. You have your political enemies encouraging citizens to not accept you as the legitimate ruler. You have every justification you need to compel your followers to fight for you. They are willing to fight and die for you. Now is the time to have them act before they view you as a weak leader."

"Yes, you are absolutely right. Now is the right time to bring this nation to her knees. I have a strong military that can wipe out any forces that refuse to accept my rule."

"Not so quick Dominik. We want this to be drawn out over a long time. The longer your nation is in turmoil the more likely the rest of the world will look elsewhere for leadership. That is how I will make Russia great again!"

"Yes, I will do as you wish tovarisch Porchensky."

"Your father taught you respect after all. Maybe we can teach you some Russian one day."

"He did not want me to have an accent or accidentally use the language in public, so he refrained from teaching me too much Russian as a child."

"What a shame. It is such a beautiful language. Okay, Dominik, I must get some rest. I will have an agent backfill you on our latest intelligence report tomorrow. Make sure he has clearance to get into the White House."

"I suppose I should get to work preparing our military to be ready for war. Before I go, I want to invite you to my second inauguration ceremony in two weeks. We must send a message to the world of who the United States of America views as an ally. It is time to create the great Russian-American alliance."

"Yes, that is a novel idea! Now you are showing courage of conviction. Count me in! The world will not know what hit them when they witness a Russian president at an American president's inauguration ceremony. A glorious new day is upon us!"

MESSAGE OF DIVISION

January 7th-8th, 2021

In the forty-eight hours after the nation went dark, President Vil had constructed much of his plan. Over the course of those hours, several advisors and government officials had tendered their resignations. They wanted nothing to do with Vil and the coming crisis. Nevertheless, his core team of advisors remained steadfast at his side as they developed a plan to stop any more uprisings.

His national security advisor updated him on the status of his desire to arrest his political opponents. He had formulated a plan that would allow federal agents to arrest anyone that they suspected of terrorism and hold them indefinitely. The plan would allow them to remove the president's opponents to overseas military installations.

This would prevent his opponents from receiving any press coverage and deny them access to legal counsel for the time being. This pleased President Vil very much. He did not care if he detained innocent parties, he simply wanted to disrupt any potential attempt to remove him from power. The next step in the plan called for the construction of several detention centers to be built all over the nation.

These detention centers would serve to hold citizens suspected of sedition, terrorism, or other acts against the federal government. The plan called for the construction of almost one hundred large detention centers, with the potential to hold upwards of one million Americans. He argued for the construction of more detention centers if they needed them in the future.

The national security advisor informed the president that this was the projected number of Americans they believed would be party to any uprising. President Vil believed the number might be higher but was given assurance that there was more noise and bluster than there was courage of conviction. He concurred with the plan and authorized it to begin.

He then authorized the mobilization of all military forces to be prepared to defend the homeland. His son-in-law was now carrying out his military orders after the entire military leadership and defense secretary had resigned the previous month after his refusal to concede the election. He had his military leaders replaced with loyalists that were willing to carry out his orders.

The directives the new military commanders gave, instructed all military members to pledge allegiance to their commander-in-chief and to comply with his orders. They instructed their subordinates to have every member of the military sign a loyalty pledge document within three days' time. If they refused, they would be detained and sent to one of the detention centers.

To continue his path of chaos, he authorized the immediate closure of both the northern and southern borders, the termination of all international inbound flights, and the denial of any inbound maritime passenger vessels. Although this would leave thousands of Americans stranded outside the nation, his desire was to send a clear message that he was in charge and would not stand down.

The only problem with his strategy is that there was no way to disseminate his message to the citizens. The nation was in the dark, with only intermittent power in places with generators. He always relied on using the press or social media to his advantage, but now most of the nation would not know the actions he was taking to do what he believed would secure the nation. Publicity, no matter how bad, was how he excelled.

To further disrupt his plans, in less than twenty-four hours after the nation was cast into the dark, the power had suddenly been restored for a short time. In what was less than a ten minute speech, Governor Perez appeared all over the television, social media channels, and the internet to send a second message to the nation. He interpreted her message as one of treason and again called for her arrest.

As a pure act of loyalty, President Vil easily convinced the remaining members of Congress to grant him emergency powers to conduct wartime operations on American soil. Several of the loyal politicians did not want to see the nation placed under military rule due to civil unrest, so they placed a stipulation into the law. They required that an attack on the nation must occur for the law to go into effect.

This placed a limitation on President Vil's powers. It was a limited effort to display some form of congressional power. However, he was already formulating a plan to create a fake attack against the nation to allow him the emergency wartime powers.

The power remained out throughout most of the capital region. Only a few federal installations were operating with generators. Vil demanded a quick response to restore power to the nation's three power grids. He felt incomplete without being able to communicate his message directly to the American people.

CHAPTER 4

MUTINY

Atticus Augustus was Conrad's younger brother. His formal navy title was Commander Atticus Augustus. He had been out to sea since the middle of December 2020. He is stationed onboard the U.S.S. Franklin D. Roosevelt, the newest and most state-of-the-art Arleigh-Burke Class Destroyer in the Navy's fleet and the third ship to bear the name. He serves as the second in command of the ship, also known as the executive officer, or XO for short. Since reporting to the ship and taking the role of XO, he witnessed the morale of the crew drop to the lowest he had ever seen in his naval career. The tense environment throughout all of 2020 took its toll on the crew of the ship just like it had all over the nation.

It did not take him long to determine the main cause of the problems onboard the ship. Commander Erikson, the ship's commanding officer conducted himself in a manner that gave Atticus the impression he was not an effective leader. This was reaffirmed after several interactions where Commander Erikson dismissed recommendations from his senior leadership, a failure to provide mentorship and career development for his officers, and a lack of transparency in his decision-making process. He also lacked trust in the crew, was a poor communicator of his strategy, assigned blame for crew failures, and was inconsistent in his instructions.

The last few months had been a true test of his patience and resilience. Several senior officers had confided in him their own concerns about Commander Erikson and his growing hostility toward the political system in the closing days of the presidential election. He had made it clear to his senior officers and to Atticus that President Vil was the only leader that could keep the Russians and Chinese on the defensive.

The uncertainty and chaos that ensued following the election only seemed to make things worse for Commander Erikson's state of mind. He became increasingly hostile toward members of the crew. He made the crew work long hours so they would have little free time to interact with the local population after their workday. The nation had been put on edge after the election and the ongoing pandemic, and Commander Erikson wanted the crew to remain out of the fray. He issued an order that only allowed them to go directly to their homes when they were not on the ship.

His prayers had been delivered when his request for their ship to serve as the west coast patrol ship during the holidays was granted. It was an unusual position for the Navy to have a vessel at sea during the holidays unless on an overseas deployment. With tensions at an all-time high, the crew was even more disgruntled to be away from their family for the holidays. After three weeks of patrolling the coast, the crew had become increasingly skeptical of the patriotism of their captain. He made daily announcements to the crew that their loyalty is to the order of the president and that the election outcome is not a matter of dispute.

Atticus felt he could no longer support the decisions the captain made but was not ready to act in a manner inconsistent with his role as a naval officer. After dinner, on the evening of January 6th, the next three senior officers approached his cabin to discuss their concerns.

"Commander Augustus, do you have a moment?" asked Lieutenant Jack Birksby, the ship's operations officer.

"Of course I do Jack, I'm just reviewing some documents. Come on in," replied Atticus.

In walked the Lieutenant, along with the other two officers. Atticus did not realize that Jack was not alone when he had requested to speak with him. But he saw the look on their faces and knew it was urgent.

"Please, take a seat," stated Atticus, gesturing to the couch in the cabin. "From the look on your faces, this seems important."

Lieutenant Birksby closed the door to the cabin after the two other officers entered and took their seats on the couch. He remained standing, as was common for him when he was on edge.

"Atticus, I need to confide something with you that we just encountered with the captain."

"Is this something I should be alarmed about?"

"I believe so."

"Okay, you have my full attention."

"We were giving our nightly updates to the captain. His television was on the news and on mute like normal and he was only half paying attention to us. I was in the middle of giving him my update when he abruptly stood up and unmuted the television. We all looked in that direction to see Governor Perez appearing to give a press conference but as we listened to her speech, we heard her declare President Vil to be an illegitimate president and demanded his removal from office. I'm fairly confident that we heard her demand the American people unite to force him to leave office."

"Wait right there. You are telling me that a governor demanded the president to leave office and she announced that on live television?"

"Yes, it was on live television. I think our private conversations about our worst fears about the future are becoming reality. That isn't the worst part though."

"How could it possibly get worse than that?"

"After she was done talking the news feed went blank. I think the three of us were in shock, but the look on the captain's face…it was as if he was expecting something like this to happen. He mentioned something about an earlier attack on the capitol to restore power to the president.

"He was just mumbling and roaming his cabin back and forth as if we were not there. Then he radioed back to fleet headquarters for directions on how to proceed since we are the only ship at sea in the Pacific Ocean. That's when things got very eerie."

"How so?" Atticus asked.

"He radioed them at least a dozen times; there was no response, just static. Then he got on the ship's satellite phone system to contact the admiral's cell phone. He told us the call would not connect. He said that the other end of the connection was dead."

Atticus believed he knew what had happened. The last conversation he had with his brother Conrad was weeks ago. Conrad had told him that his conversation with Governor Perez was a failure and she did not believe anything could be done to force President Vil from office. Something must have occurred since then that changed her mind and he assumed his brother was involved.

Conrad must have changed the governor's mind and she decided that someone in political leadership must act. His heart began to beat heavily. He knew his brother was involved and would have answers for what they were planning and how Atticus could help. He did not want to convey his own feelings to his fellow officers or his interactions with his brother. So he simply continued to ask questions as if he did not know what was happening.

"What did the captain do after his call did not connect?" he asked.

"Well that is the worst part. He told us that we need to be prepared as the active patrol ship to assist the Coast Guard. We have to be prepared to stop any naval vessels from reaching land. He directed us to head toward the coast, directly off the coast of Los Angeles."

"Why Los Angeles?"

"He believes that will put us in the best position since the majority of commercial vessel traffic on the west coast comes in and out of the two ports located there. He wants us to remain there until we are given further direction once we can contact headquarters. He ended by telling us to get ready for the president to call on the armed forces in response to this and that he will use us to end the violence that has been going on in the streets."

Just then the desk phone in Atticus's cabin rang startling him and the other officers. He looked at the other officers in the room unsure of who would be calling his cabin phone this late in the night. He picked up the phone.

"XO," he answered, using the abbreviation referring to his title.

"Get up here right away. I have some important information that just came in."

The phone clicked. There was no need for the individual on the other end of the line to identify himself. The voice was deep and distinct. It was his commanding officer. The hair on the back of Atticus's neck stood up after hearing that voice. He was not ready to confront the man after hearing this heart wrenching news and still processing what it all meant.

"That was the captain, he wants to see me. Look, I know we do not agree with him about politics. I know he has been growing very frustrated with all the uncertainty and violence in the streets. These are dark times we are living in now, but we have to continue to follow all lawful orders given to us whether we agree with them or not. Go back to your staterooms for now and I will give an update once I know more."

THE DISGRUNTLED CAPTAIN

Atticus walked up the one flight of stairs, down the passageway and around the corner, dreading the moment he would reach his destination. That short walk was all that separated him from his commanding officer; a simple twenty second walk. He knew that specifically because he counted it on numerous occasions as he was always being called in for meetings and to answer for actions of the crew. When he arrived at the captain's cabin, he adjusted his uniform and then knocked on the door.

"Enter!" yelled the commanding officer.

Atticus turned the knob and peeked in the cabin. The captain was sitting at his desk appearing to be reading a document.

"Come in Atticus. Close the door and take a seat. There have been some major events that have unfolded over the last hour and I need to update you."

"Is this regarding our current operations?"

"No. Well, sort of. You know I have been concerned that this crazy younger generation would not accept our president as our legitimate leader no matter the outcome of the election. It appears that my concern was warranted. Tonight, there was a declaration by the governor of California to not accept our president as the legitimate ruler—"

"You mean leader, sir?"

"Excuse me?"

"I believe you simply misspoke. I think what you meant to say is that the governor does not recognize him as the legitimate leader. He does not rule over us, sir. He is an elected official, not an autocrat."

Commander Erikson took a moment to examine Atticus's response. He gleaned from his facial expression and the look in his eyes that he was not happy with how this discussion had started.

"Yes, I meant leader. Well, she has called for our citizens to take up arms and remove our president from power. After I heard this, I attempted to contact the mainland for instruction from the fleet. I was unable to make contact after several attempts."

"That seems very odd. Is there an issue with our communications systems?"

"No, it is the mainland. The nation appears to have gone dark."

"What? How is that possible?"

"They must have attacked our country from within."

"Who exactly is the 'they' that you speak of sir?" Atticus asked with an accusatory tone.

"It is the pesky governor and her liberal elite friends. They want to see our nation fall and make our great leader fail."

"I see, and how is it that you know this or is this just something you are assuming?"

"I do not have time to entertain these questions. The Pentagon is working on emergency generators and we have just received the first message they have sent to all units. Here, take a look and see for yourself."

IMMEDIATE – National Command Authority
FROM: Acting Secretary of Defense
TO: All Units

This message is to alert all units that the nation's
power grids have been disabled. The cause is
unknown but suspected to be an act of domestic
terrorism. All units are to remain alert. Relay any
priority messages immediately via any possible
means to your direct reporting senior. If immediate or
flash message, relay directly to National Command
Authority. Await further instructions.

"This is serious. What do you plan to do?"

"I have already directed the ship to head south so we can
position ourselves off the coast of Los Angeles. I believe that
puts us in a better place as a naval asset."

"What makes Los Angeles so important?"

"It is the largest city on the west coast. If there is any sort
of domestic terrorist attack out here, it will most likely
happen there. Since the nation is in the dark, there is no one
monitoring any sea or air traffic in or out of the region. We
may be the only asset on the west coast right now that can
fend off a terrorist attack by sea or air."

"Do you want to alert the crew?"

"No, not yet. It is too late at night. I will make an announcement in the morning."

"Very well, sir. Is there anything you want me to do?"

"Yes there is. I need you to make sure that the officers understand their oath. We swore an oath. If the president issues any orders, we are to carry them out. Their personal opinions and beliefs do not matter."

"Y--yes sir. I understand. Try and get some rest. We have a long day ahead of us tomorrow."

Atticus returned to his cabin. He felt his heart sink. This was going to be a true test of his character. The crew would not take the news well in the morning. He remembered on numerous occasions when fellow officers told him of the rumblings amongst the crew.

First, it was how they were not confident in their commanding officer because of the way he treated them. Then, it was how the country had been tricked by a president, their own commander-in-chief, to manipulate the Constitution and remain in power. Now, he was being faced with the captain preparing the crew for what will be very dark days ahead, and that their loyalty was to carry out an illegitimate president's orders. Those orders may end up going against their fellow citizens; something no servicemember had been confronted with since the civil war.

On the flip side, he also knew that some crew members believed the president was fully justified in his actions to not give up the presidency. There were also a good number that did not care about politics, they simply wanted to serve their nation.

As he lie down on his bunk, he felt torn. How will the crew react to this news? Will the crew talk about the future of the nation? Will the captain voice his true feelings about those that want the president removed when he speaks to the crew just as he does in private?

It was time for him to contact his brother. If there was anyone that could confirm what is happening stateside it is Conrad. He grabbed his satellite phone, tucked it in his uniform, and headed topside to make the call. He looked around to see if anyone was around before reaching for the phone. It was almost midnight now so most of the crew was asleep. He dialed Conrad's phone.

"Damn the call isn't connecting. I guess the satellite connections are down too," he said, voicing his internal frustration out loud.

He heard a noise in the distance that startled him. Then he remembered that the noises the waves make when they hit the side of the ship always make him feel as if they hit something in the ocean. Scanning his surroundings, he saw a small light that was getting brighter and brighter. The light was a small orange glow. It could not have been larger than a quarter in size. The light kept getting closer. He saw the light brighten and then dim.

"XO, you're up quite late, don't you think?" inquired the voice as it approached.

He recognized the deep voice. It was the command master chief, the ship's senior enlisted member.

"You know...those cigars are going to kill you one day, master chief."

"The navy is going to kill me one day, sir. I reckon with what I have gone through over the last thirty years, I only have a few years left anyway. I might as well partake in the things I enjoy. Besides...the wife won't let me do it when I'm home, so I have to get them in while we are out to sea."

"Well just your luck, it looks like we might be out to sea for a while master chief."

"Yeah, I figured as much."

"Why do you say that?"

"Do you think things happen on this ship without me finding out? I knew seconds after the message came in over the wire."

"The captain is really hell bent that there is an attempted coup going on stateside. He has really been warped by the rhetoric."

"I know. I've known the man for about fifteen years. When he was a junior officer, he was a different leader than he is today. He really took his divorce hard. He started drinking heavily after that and has not been the same person since. I see him more and more consumed with political propaganda every day. When I have my meetings with him, he is sure to point out his feelings. The way I view it, we are here to serve a mission. We are to uphold the Constitution and to carry out the 'lawful' orders of those appointed over us. I just want the crew to know that whatever actions we take as a ship is within the scope of those boundaries."

"What do we do if he orders us to do something that violates our core values and goes against the Constitution?"

"Well sir, that's why they pay you the big bucks with that fancy college education. Know that I will follow and relay to the crew only lawful orders. Look, it's late, we have a long day ahead of us tomorrow. You need some rest."

"Yeah, I'll head inside in a few. I just need to get some fresh air a little longer."

Atticus gazed upon the open sky. The stars and the moon shine so bright tonight. The ocean breeze was calming. The waves sounded calm as they lightly bounced off the side of the ship. He remained outside staring into the sky for a few minutes longer, until he yawned. Atticus knew that he needed to get rest to be prepared for what he believed was going to be a long next day.

ABRUPT AWAKENING

January 7th, 2021

"Reveille! Reveille! All hands heave out and trice up. Reveille!"

Atticus shot up from his bed. He glanced at the clock across the cabin. It read: 06:00

"How can it be the morning already?" he asked himself. "I need to get ready and head to the captain's cabin to help him prepare to brief the department heads and the crew."

He quickly did his morning routine and just as he stepped out of the shower, he heard the bugle call that is played before the commanding officer makes an announcement.

"Good morning crew of the U.S.S. Franklin D. Roosevelt, this is your captain. I know that I do not normally make announcements this early in the morning, but this is very important. I want you to hear it from me first.

"Yesterday, our country experienced what may have been a massive cyber attack on the nation's power grids. As of right now, the entire nation is without power. Thankfully, we have been able to make limited communication with the fleet and our nation's top military commanders. It appears that this was a coordinated attempt to undermine our duly elected president.

"Last night, preceding the cyber attack, the governor of California addressed the nation in what we suspect to be a call to arms against the nation. It appears there have been several political opponents of our commander-in-chief that want him removed from power...by force, if necessary. The military has been ordered to be on high alert for any possible attack on bases and ships.

"We were directed to proceed off the coast of Los Angeles to patrol and protect the region against any potential air or sea attack. For security reasons you will find that there are no off-ship communications for the time being. Not that you would be able to utilize any communications given the lack of power stateside. I know this is incredibly hard to hear right now. Let me just remind everyone that we took an oath and that oath is to protect our nation against all enemies foreign and domestic. That is all."

"What is he doing?" Atticus questioned. "He is going to have the crew on edge. There is already enough tension aboard the ship, this was not the way to announce this."

Atticus finished getting dressed and headed for the bridge. On his way, he recognized the look of a beaten down crew. As he approached several members of the crew enroute to the bridge, he heard the whisperings that immediately stopped when they recognized their XO approaching. He saw the look of concern on their faces. He arrived at the bridge and took a deep breath.

"Good morning, captain. May I have a word?"

"Of course. Let's step out onto the starboard bridge wing," he said, gesturing for Atticus to follow him outside.

"Sir, are you sure that your announcement was the best way to inform the crew?"

"They needed to know before the rumors started going around the ship."

"I agree with you, but you told them that there are political leaders within our government that are attempting a coup on our president. Then you told them that we, as military professionals, are to remain loyal to our president."

"Well, it does appear to be a coup. And our loyalty is to our president."

"With all due respect, our loyalty is to the Constitution. We are to obey all lawful orders given to us."

"Look Atticus, I'm not going to get into a legal argument with you. We have been ordered off the coast of Los Angeles and we will obey all orders given to us.

"I thought you said you wanted to position the ship off the coast of Los Angeles. Now you are saying we were ordered there."

"Early this morning, we received a maritime patrol alert. The CIA suspects several China flagged container ships headed toward the west coast, to arrive in the next few days. They assess that some of them are headed toward Los Angeles. We have been directed to track them down, stop them as soon as they reach U.S. territorial waters, and board them."

"Okay, but container ships go in and out of Los Angeles every day. What makes these ships worth tracking?"

"They are believed to have military weapons onboard. They are being delivered to arm the anti-U.S. militias."

"When are we expected to arrive near the Los Angeles coast?"

"Approximately 2100 hours."

"Very well sir. I will brief the department heads."

MUTINY IN THE AIR

Atticus updated the department heads on the current situation as he knew it. He was concerned they would have questions that he could not answer. To his surprise, the first question was something he was worried was time to confront.

"Atticus, I think we can all be open here. This is a safe space to talk right?" asked Lieutenant Birksby.

"I always hold our conversations to be private. What you confide with me stays here," replied Atticus.

"Well let me be the first to speak my mind. You know I'm not much of a political person, in fact I didn't even vote this last time. But I also believe that what the president did to trash the Constitution in some last-ditch effort to maintain his grip on power was not only unconstitutional but threatens our democracy.

"I believe the people are simply standing up to let their voices be heard. They have a legitimate right to do so. I do not think it is in the interests of the military to get involved in the domestic matters of our nation. The president made his choice and now the people are making theirs."

Those words caught Atticus off guard. He always knew Lieutenant Birksby to be an apolitical person. The other department heads nodded in agreement with the lieutenant.

"What do you believe we should do?" asked Atticus.

"That's a tricky question. We have not been ordered to do anything illegal, unconstitutional or against our core values. At least not yet. I suppose we have no choice but to continue this mission for now. I remain worried that we may get asked to get involved in whatever is going on stateside and asked to intervene. I think I stand alongside my fellow department heads…and frankly much of the crew, when I say that would be a step too far."

"I hear you. So you believe the crew is not onboard with what we have been tasked to do?"

"Have you not heard the talk around the ship? There are a good number of the crew that believe what happened after the election is unconstitutional and are very unhappy with the response the president ordered to squash the protestors. A lot of the crew believes he is not the legitimately elected president, but they are afraid to voice their opinions too loudly since we are supposed to be non-partisan as military members."

"I have heard some talk around the ship. I overhear more complaints about the commanding officer than anything."

"Yes, he is clearly a supporter of the president and is willing to use whatever force we can to end these protests."

"Alright, let us all continue about our day. Keep me apprised of any issues you encounter. We will get back to this later."

COMMUNICATION RESTORED

Atticus arrived in the officer's wardroom at the end of the lunch hour to avoid any conversations about the unfolding events. He quietly ate his lunch and then headed back to his cabin. When he sat down at his desk, he noticed his satellite phone on his desk.

"What are the odds that the cell phone towers are working back stateside?" he pondered to himself.

He decided to grab his phone and head up to the signal house, located behind the bridge. It was the only location on the ship he could avoid an encounter and safely make a call during the day.

When he got to the signal house, he carefully scanned his surroundings before pulling his satellite phone out. He dialed Conrad's secure line. This time, to his surprise, the phone rang.

"Hello little brother. How are you holding up out there?" asked Conrad.

"I cannot believe we have a connection right now. I heard the whole nation went dark."

"I have so much to fill you in on. I'm sorry I have not communicated with you in so long. I wish I had time to discuss everything that has occurred over the last few weeks, but I don't know how long we will have this connection. You actually got really lucky with this call, I just so happened to be outside while the power is on. We have been so busy preparing for our next move."

"Okay, so if you don't have time to tell me everything, just give me the short and sweet."

"Several of the nation's governors no longer recognize President Vil as the legitimate president. They have called for his resignation and he has refused. We have begun the process to force him from power with the help of the people. Today alone we already have hundreds of thousands of people fleeing to our resistance locations to join the movement. Americans want to fight to save this country. Look, we have a plan, that if executed properly, will remove him from office and allow the nation to return to peace."

"What do you need me to do, brother?"

"We have weapons and supplies arriving in several places on the west coast to support this mission. I don't think our side understands how easily these shipments can be tracked—"

"We already know about the shipments. Our ship has been directed to stop them before they arrive."

"Then we need you to do whatever you can to allow those shipments to make it to their destination. Our forces will stand no match against the U.S. military without the aid that those shipments will provide."

"You know that my commanding officer will do anything he can to be an active participant in crushing the resistance. He wants us to find and stop those cargo ships."

"Then you have to stop him! If that means you commit mutiny, then so be it!"

"That is not even a possibility. I would have to get the crew onboard with that."

"I'm sure you will find a way. We don't have much time before the connections go down again so I need to get this information to you quickly. I suspect that most of the fleet will be ordered to sea within the next few days. President Vil will use those assets to bombard every major population center to show his strength and get as many people to walk away from our mission. We cannot let him get those ships out to sea. We have no one on the east coast, but we have you on the west, and we need you to—"

The line went dead. Atticus attempted to call his brother back but there was no use, the connection was lost. The power grid must have gone down again.

"What in the hell is going on?" he asked himself. "How am I supposed to allow these cargo ships to make it to port?"

"XO to the bridge," announced the voice over the ship's communication system.

"Oh great, now the captain wants to talk to me," he thought. Reluctantly, he stepped around the corner and into the bridge to find the commanding officer waiting for him, grinning from ear to ear.

"I have something that you need to disperse to the department heads. The entire crew needs to sign these forms within 24 hours," stated Commander Erikson while handing Atticus a copy of the form that the president issued earlier in the day demanding loyalty from his military.

Quickly glancing at the document, he knew it was best to avoid confrontation with his commanding officer for now. He replied, "I will look this over and get it to the department heads so that we can have the crew sign it."

Atticus left the bridge and down the three flights to find the operations officer, his friend Lieutenant Jack Birksby, in his stateroom. He immediately noticed the frustration on Atticus's face.

"What's wrong?" he asked.

"Look at this," he said, handing him the form. "This came in just now. It is a pledge of loyalty that everyone must sign. It looks like it came from the president. I imagine that this form has been dispersed to the entire military. The president is demanding our loyalty to him and him alone."

"This will not go over well with the officers or the crew. Is this even legal?"

"I don't think so but what can we do? He wants the entire crew to sign them by this time tomorrow."

"This may be the tipping point, XO. If the president is going to demand that the armed services pledge loyalty to him then we do not have a commander-in-chief anymore. I'm not one to wage into the waters of doing something against regulations, but this has my blood boiling."

Atticus felt now was his best chance to tell his friend Jack of what Conrad told him. Maybe he could convince him to join their side. If it backfired, then it would most likely mean confinement to his cabin. He decided to just go for it and he told Jack everything that he knew.

"Wow! This is crazy! So, your brother is working with the California governor, several of President Vil's political enemies and a bunch of militia groups to conduct a coup?"

"It is not a coup, and there are now hundreds of thousands that have joined their ranks in just a few hours. This president did not adhere to the will of the people. He is turning our country into an autocracy and that is not something that I am willing to let happen."

"What do you plan to do?"

"I will confront the captain and tell him that what he has asked of the crew is unconstitutional, unpatriotic, and goes against our core values. If he continues to demand that we sign the document, then I will have no choice but to ask for him to step aside as the commanding officer for carrying out an unlawful order and for betrayal of the Constitution."

"And what if your plan fails?"

"Then I go to court martial and it will be the end of my career. But that is not what is important right now. This is a moment where we must stand on our principles. We have a choice to stand up for our nation when she needs us most or we can very quickly see an end to everything that our predecessors signed up for and so many gave their lives for. I need to know if you are in this."

Atticus felt the tension as Jack looked deep into his eyes. Time seemed to freeze as he awaited Jack's response.

"Okay...I'm in. This will probably end up not working, but you remind me of my parents. They were both teachers and I spent countless hours at the dinner table being lectured about patriotism. That's how I ended up here. We have to do the right thing. We will ask him to rescind his order and if he refuses then we confine him to his quarters."

"We have to convince the other department heads."

"Leave that up to me. They should all come around. We might have an issue with the weapons officer but let me see what I can do. What about the crew?"

"I'll talk to the command master chief. He seems to understand what it means to be a patriot. Not everyone will be with us. For those that aren't, we can isolate them together to a berthing on the ship."

Atticus spent the next hour developing his plan, then he briefed the command master chief. To his surprise, the command master chief conveyed his own concerns that he believed it was only a matter of time before something of this nature occurred. He told Atticus that he wouldn't let anyone in the crew stand in the way as long as he gave the captain a chance to come around. Conrad agreed and then retired to his cabin for the night.

CONFRONTATION

January 8th, 2021

Atticus woke up bright and early before the reveille call. He got dressed and headed to Lieutenant Birksby's stateroom where he found the majority of department heads waiting for him, minus the weapons officer who had still not been briefed on the plan. He updated them on how he intended to proceed and gave them the opportunity to back out. None of them did. They headed for the commanding officer's cabin. He told the others to stand outside and then he knocked on the door.

"Sir, do you have a moment?"

"Yes, of course I do. You are up here a little earlier than usual. We are not supposed to have our morning meeting for another hour. Were you able to get the signatures from the crew giving their loyalty to the president?"

"That's what I came to talk to you about. Sir, this document is a flagrant violation of our Constitution. It requests that we pledge our loyalty to the president. Nowhere in here does it tell us to pledge our loyalty to the Constitution. That is what we swore to uphold, not some disgruntled president who lost his re-election bid and is making every last feasible attempt to hold onto power."

"You better be careful with your words. You are on the verge of using words treasonous to our commander-in-chief."

"No sir, that is where you are wrong. We pledge our loyalty to the Constitution not to a person. When someone leverages the power of their office to refute the will of the people then that person has committed treason. I came here to ask you to rescind the order you gave me to have the crew betray the Constitution and their oaths in order to sign this document."

"And if I do not?"

"Then I have no choice but to relieve you of command and have you confined to your quarters."

"For what? This is ridiculous. You want to relieve me of command for following the order of the president and to defend this nation against domestic terrorists? These unpatriotic citizens are destroying our way of life!"

"No sir. For treason against the Constitution, the nation, and the Navy regulations. Sir, somewhere along the way you forgot your oath. You do not swear an oath to one individual. Your oath is to the Constitution and to maintaining the republic. You are betraying your oath and for that I have no other option but to relieve you of command and order you confined to quarters." Gesturing outside to the department heads, he continued, "Gentlemen, remove any means of communication from the captain's cabin and get the master-at-arms up here to stand guard. I will make an announcement to the crew."

SIGNAL

"Crew of the U.S.S. Franklin D. Roosevelt, this is Commander Augustus," he started his announcement to the crew over the ship's speaker system. "I have relieved Commander Erikson of his duties as commanding officer for disloyalty to the United States. I have taken command of the ship under U.S. Navy regulations.

"Crew, we are experiencing tumultuous times. The nation is currently divided between those that recognize our commander-in-chief as the legitimate and duly elected leader and those that believe he has committed an act treasonous to our Constitution. While I cannot tell you how to believe…that is a decision you have to make within your own heart. What I can tell you is that from this day forward, this ship…the Franklin D. Roosevelt, will stand true to the name bestowed upon her.

"If you feel that I have made the wrong choice by relieving Commander Erikson, then I will give you the next thirty minutes to find your way to the hangar bay. You will be removed from the ship and taken to shore. No one will be charged with any article against the UCMJ. You will simply be allowed to go ashore after being relieved of your duties. If you choose to stay aboard, know that your nation is calling you to stand up for her. She needs patriotic Americans to fight to save her from tyranny. Your nation needs you now more than ever!"

Atticus remained on the bridge giving instructions to the officer of the deck to immediately notify him if they identify the suspected China-flagged cargo ships. He intended to ensure their safe passage to port. When he was notified that the crew members not willing to remain aboard were gathered in the hangar bay, he left the bridge to see them off.

When he arrived, he was told there were 93 officers and crew assembled. That meant about a third of the crew was assembled in the hangar bay ready to be taken to shore. This number was greater than he expected, but he had no choice but to send them ashore.

Several lifeboats were dropped into the water and the assembled crew members climbed down a ladder one by one and boarded the lifeboats. They were escorted by the ship's rescue boat to San Nicolas Island, a small, unmanned island off the coast of Los Angeles used by the Navy as a weapons testing facility. Commander Erikson was among the crew forced off the ship.

Atticus spend much of the remainder of the day speaking with the remaining members of the crew to explain his actions further. He wanted to gain their trust since he believed there might be a few members of the crew remaining onboard that were not fully persuaded by his actions but also did not want to leave the ship.

The crew continued to monitor the waters and radar for the suspected cargo ships. They had not been given any indication of when the ships would arrive off the coast. Atticus believed that they would appear in a formation of ships rather than separately. There was no evidence to back this up, but he believed the ships would stay close together to better fend off an attack.

Just before sunset Atticus stepped out onto the port bridge wing. He gazed off into the sunset for a few moments. Tonight the sun appeared incredibly large as it escaped behind the ocean surface off in the distance. That is when he noticed a glare from an object in the distance right in the sun's path. He grabbed his binoculars to get a better look.

"Officer of the deck, I believe I see three vessels on our port side, bearing 280, just along the horizon. Can you see if we hold them on radar?"

"Yes, I do see what appears to be three vessels in that location about nine nautical miles out," replied the officer of the deck on watch.

Atticus gave the order to turn the ship in the direction of the oncoming vessels to confirm they were the ships they were looking to intercept. As they made their approach, they were able to identify all three as China-flagged cargo ships. He radioed the ships, identifying themselves. They did not respond. After several attempts to reach them, he gave the order to send the rescue boat to board the lead ship.

He sent seven crew members over as a boarding team to the lead cargo ship. They conducted their initial safety sweep, then tied alongside the cargo ship, five of them boarded the ship. They proceeded cautiously to the bridge. The boarding team officer in charge radioed back that the ship appeared to have no one onboard. Atticus cautioned them to remain alert as they entered the bridge.

They approached the bridge, breached the door, conducting a tactical entry. They discovered four men in coveralls on the bridge. The cargo ship's captain identified himself, but no one spoke English. The lead officer radioed back to the ship for their linguist to get on the radio.

Their linguist was able to gather from the conversation with the cargo ship's captain that they were unaware of the contents of their shipment. They were only given directions to proceed to Los Angeles and arrive no later than January 8th to unload their cargo.

Atticus had his linguist explain to their captain that they would escort them into port. The captain questioned the purpose a naval warship would escort three cargo ships into port. He did not want to alarm the crew of the cargo ship if they were truthful about not knowing what was onboard.

Atticus told his linguist to relay the following message, "The United States has experienced a major nationwide power outage and requires all incoming vessels to be escorted into port until further notice."

They escorted the ships into the Port of Los Angeles, arriving early the following morning. Atticus believed they would remain at sea for a significant amount of time, so he directed the ship to moor alongside the pier ahead of the cargo ships. This would allow them to monitor the safe offload and use the time to replenish their fuel and load food onto their ship.

As they pulled alongside the pier, Atticus noticed what he believed to be about seventy to eighty men and women in military style uniforms waiting at the far end of the pier. He used his binoculars to get a better look. Sure enough these men and women were dressed in military style uniforms that appeared to be outdated uniforms that had long been replaced by newer, more digitally designed ones.

He scanned the group to determine who this group might be associated with. There was an expectation that the cargo ships would be greeted with members of the newly formed resistance forces, but he could not just assume that this group was indeed the forces he expected. His eyes caught the attention of a woman not in a military uniform, something that stood out in the sea of uniforms. The woman was tall, with dark skin, her hair pulled into a bun, wearing dark trousers with a matching jacket, and sunglasses to shield her eyes from the bright sun.

He continued to observe the woman, believing that she looked familiar to him. He could not quite pinpoint why it triggered his memory. Then she removed her sunglasses and Atticus knew why she had a familiar appearance.

The woman that stood on the pier with the men and women in uniform was Jasmine Williams, his brother's former colleague. She had spent a lot of time at Conrad's house when Atticus was a junior officer. Back then she had just left the Navy to pursue college and start a career on her own. Atticus began to develop feelings for her and they briefly dated. They never told Conrad because they both believed he would not approve of his younger brother and his former colleague dating. After a few months of dating, Atticus received orders to the Pentagon and Jasmine had just opened a cybersecurity firm, so they both decided to end the relationship.

"Well, my brother surely wanted to make sure this operation didn't go south," he thought, "but why did he have to send her?"

After the ship moored, he directed his supply officer to work with the port authority to replenish their fuel and to procure at least three months' worth of food. He gave him a ten-hour deadline for them to procure their replenishments for the ship so they could get back to sea before sunset. After issuing his directive, Atticus left the ship to look for Jasmine. She was at the next pier, overseeing the offload from the first cargo ship.

"Hello Jasmine, it has been far too long."

"And who's fault is that?" she asked, "If I do recall, you left for D.C. and I never heard from you again."

"I guess I have an apology to make. I felt it was best to move on. You really left an impression on me. If we had maintained any form of communication, I do not know that I could have ever moved on. Can you find it in your heart to forgive me?"

Jasmine gazed into his eyes to determine if he was sincere. She replied, "Look, we do not have time to rehash old wounds. We have a mission to complete and a very tight timeline."

"I suppose my brother sent you."

"Yes, but before you think this has anything to do with you, it doesn't. I was put in charge of this operation by General Hamilton directly. Conrad only learned of it yesterday. He told me that your ship had been tasked with preventing the shipments from getting to port. He believed the only way they would make it was if you succeeded in relieving your captain. I guess you are into acts of mutiny these days."

"It's not mutiny if we did it for the survival of the nation and democracy itself."

"Well, then we need to take back the country from this dictator quickly. If things don't work out along our timeline then this could turn into a stalemate, which won't work out well for us. We are outnumbered and so a first strike is our best option."

"What is the plan? I have been in the dark on this. Until yesterday I had not spoken with Conrad in almost a month. This must have been a quickly developed plan."

"I've never seen something developed in such a short timeline. The plan is to remove him from power before he is sworn in for a second term. We cannot allow him the symbology of standing at the Capitol being legitimized as the president and commander-in-chief."

"So how are we going to stop him? What is the plan?"

Jasmine briefed Atticus on the details of Operation Fire Storm.

"So he wants me to take the ship down to San Diego and prevent the ships from making it to sea? That is only about a third of the fleet."

"Yes, but that is a third of the fleet that we won't have to worry about being able to be used as assets against our forces. We have no Navy…we just have your ship. We need you to prevent them from making it to sea."

"We get underway this evening after we take on our shipments. I'm assuming they will be setting to sea within the next few days."

"We believe they will embark within the next two days. They are in the process of recalling everyone back to the bases and are preparing the ships for sea."

"That gives us a little time to develop our plan."

Atticus and Jasmine continued discussing Operation Fire Storm, working through possible scenarios and outcomes. He gave Jasmine a few ideas to take back to Conrad, as backup plans if the operation failed.

"Oh, one more thing before you go. You know how we both agreed to keep our relationship a secret from Conrad?" Jasmine asked.

"He would have never approved of his younger brother dating his colleague."

"Well, it turns out he knew the entire time. He was disappointed when you took orders to the Pentagon and we called it quits."

"How did he even know? He never said anything to me."

"I asked him that same question. In his typical fashion he said it was his big brother's intuition."

They spoke their farewells and wished each other success. The sun had set and the ship had been replenished in record time, with fuel and several months' worth of food supply. The cargo ships continued to be offloaded as the U.S.S. Franklin D. Roosevelt set back to sea.

CHAPTER 5

FIRST STRIKE

G eneral Hamilton had just returned from two days of meetings with his billionaire casino tycoon friend. While he was there, he met with several other billionaires to secure additional funding. Some of them were skeptical of the potential for success and refused to commit during his visit. There were also several billionaires that were optimistic given General Hamilton's history of success during the Iraq and Afghanistan wars, so they committed some financial aid to fund their operation.

His greatest success came in the form of an offer from a hedge fund executive that had connections to arms dealers all over the world. He offered to provide military equipment and weapons to be delivered to the east coast. General Hamilton was quite relieved by that offer since they had been unable to secure any support from the European Union or any other nation to provide support for their factions outside of the west coast.

Although they had planned for a quick operation, the likelihood that President Vil would quickly step down was still unknown. Being able to provide the necessary military weapons would ensure their back up plan had a greater likelihood of success. After the funding was secured, General Hamilton returned to the Sierra Nevada headquarters by motorcade, opting to avoid any possible detection by air.

Immediately following the two days of meetings, most of the billionaires fled to their private underground bunkers, spread throughout the nation, to safely avoid the pending conflict. There were a few more optimistic billionaires that chose to remain in Las Vegas, believing there would be little direct impact after the operation. The rest of them went to find refuge at their vacation homes in isolated and remote regions of the country.

Upon his return, General Hamilton informed Rosa, Conrad, and the other generals about the success in Las Vegas. He would have preferred to have secured more monetary assistance but was pleased to have procured military weapons that would be shipped to their forces on the east coast. There were many problems that had arisen while he was gone that had still not been resolved.

Rosa was very concerned with their inability to communicate with each site since they had taken down the power grids. Their primary means of communication was through drones that relayed visual footage through encrypted battery powered relay stations. They also relied on messengers to personally relay messages between sites. Everyone agreed their secondary means of communication was insufficient.

Conrad proposed a series of radio relay stations to communicate amongst their factions. This could prove to be tricky and very time consuming. It would require they set up each relay station along a route between sites. Each relay station would need to be positioned no further than forty miles due to the distance limits of radio wave transmission.

He could easily encrypt the transmissions like he did with the drones. They were not sure if they could install enough relay stations in the few days they had remaining. They had thousands of miles to cover in all directions. Their resistance sites were located all over the nation, spread out in remote locations. His proposal would allow them to communicate quicker and more reliably than through messengers, but they also agreed they were constrained with time.

They also argued over the lack of food resources. Most grocery stores did not have generators and those that did, were limited in what they could allocate their generator power supply toward. Food was beginning to spoil and stores had been ransacked as civilians began to hoard whatever food and water was available to them. They had accounted for a significant drop in the food supply chain, but not to the degree and speed that they were experiencing.

Several sites had emergency food packages, also known as meals, ready-to-eat (MRE's). These were packaged containers that comprised of food rations that did not require refrigeration, which allowed for a long shelf life. They believed their current supply of MRE's would run out in less than two weeks if they did not make further reductions in rations.

Jasmine had returned with mixed news about their military weapons shipments. They had received a greater number of firearms, ammunition, and personal body armor than they expected. However, they only received half of the short and mid-range missile shipment they were promised.

The shipments that Jasmine oversaw also lacked any military vehicles. It felt to them that the Chinese gave them just enough equipment to start an operation but not enough to win one. A stalemate is what they believed the Chinese may be counting on. They would have to improvise a means of logistics and transportation to get their shipments to each of their sites.

They began to feel overwhelmed and without clear answers or guidance. Several members of the resistance, located within their headquarters had offered possible solutions, but none seemed promising. Once General Hamilton was briefed on the status, his effectiveness as their military leader became evident.

"I've only been gone a few days and things are already beginning to fall apart. Everyone seems overwhelmed, there are a lot of roadblocks we seem to have ahead of us, but we can clear them if we look for possible and realistic solutions," stated General Hamilton.

"What recommendations do you have general?" asked Rosa.

"Let's start with the communications issue. We can only monitor our drones, which provides us with real-time footage of events. It takes hours if not days for messengers to relay communication between sites. We have a major offensive that is due to occur in just a few days and our means of communication is inefficient.

"Conrad's idea to install relay stations is the best alternative, but the reality is that could take months to complete. We need to consider that we restore power, which will also resolve some of our food supply issues. As an alternative, we can intermittently restore power while conducting communication efforts. We can plan a rotating power restoration so that we do not establish a pattern that would give Vil's forces the ability to decipher when power will be restored each day. We also do not want them attempting to track our communications, so we will need to continue to scramble our encryption."

"General, I agree with your proposal, but I also believe your timeline for setting up relay stations is off significantly. The current technology allows each station to be solar powered, which will drastically reduce the time to set up each relay. Also, we do not have to recreate the wheel when it comes to this," stated Conrad.

"What exactly do you mean?" he asked.

"There is already an existing set of radio towers nationwide. It has been around for almost one hundred years. We use them to listen to music and the news every day. Those radio towers are not operational since there is no power supply, but if we install our relay devices on those towers, we should be able to communicate off the existing infrastructure."

"What about the power supply?"

"They are solar powered. The entire system is smaller than an average person and can be attached to the existing towers. This could provide us nationwide communications."

"How long do you estimate that would take to install?"

"If we get the message out today with the locations of the warehouses that already have the relay stations so they can be acquired, detailed maps of each existing radio tower, allocate responsibility for each site to cover a certain area of radio towers, dedicate manpower at each site to cover the amount of radio towers; I'd say a week to ten days at most."

"Conrad, it sounds like you have a busy day ahead of you. Get your team together, compile that information, have power restored when you are ready to transmit, and get that information out A.S.A.P. to our sites!"

Conrad immediately left the meeting to assemble his team. He left Jasmine behind since she had been involved with the shipments that arrived in Los Angeles.

"Now, we can move along to our food resources. Farmers are still tending to animals and their crop and I do not see that changing anytime soon. Yes, the lack of power will hinder some of the supply chain movement, but I have faith that they will find a way to resolve those issues on their own. I grew up on a farm…if there is anything I have learned about farmers; it is that they are resilient. They will continue to get food to their destination.

"Let's not even contemplate a scenario where we are reliant on the regular food chain. We need to consider that our only option is to rely on MRE's. There are several military supply locations that are stocked with a lifetime inventory of MRE's. Some of these locations are off-base warehouses with minimal security.

"I suggest that we obtain MRE's from these locations. They offer the least resistance to our forces. We should still send several teams just in case they have increased security. Each warehouse can easily fill twenty or more semi-trailers with MRE's and other supplies, so we need to procure semi-trucks and trailers. Colonel Inouye can provide the locations of the warehouses. We can transmit that information when Conrad has the power restored later today.

"I will work with the colonel to get the locations of those warehouses and disseminate it to the appropriate sites," Jasmine quickly volunteered.

"That works, but you and I have some work to do with this final issue regarding our weapons shipment. We need to make sure that we properly distribute all firearms, ammunition, and armor to each site. As for the missiles, we need to have direct control over them. I suggest we relocate the Los Angeles missiles to a site outside of Palm Spring for now. Once we know what arrived in Seattle and San Francisco, we can determine where to send those shipments. I have some initial ideas, but I think we should look at our maps to determine our best logistics option."

Jasmine and General Hamilton reviewed their options to move their limited missile resources. They plotted where and how to move them without brining attention to them. Jasmine was worried about the unknown consequences of starting military operations in the middle of a worldwide pandemic that had started the previous year. Thousands were dying each day and there was no end in sight.

OPERATIONS BEGIN TO MATERIALIZE

Over the next several days, things began to fall into place. Conrad successfully disseminated every known radio tower location to their forces with instructions for how to install the relay stations. Each site dispatched large numbers of forces to set up their communications network. In the meantime, they continued the plan to energize the power grids for significant communications, as necessary. As the network began to come online, they started shifting communications to the preferred method so they could leave the nation in the dark as long as possible.

They did not want to give the federal government enough time to use that uptime to track their movements. They had to assume that the government had allotted significant resources to track the resistance forces. However, they significantly outnumbered the number of agents in the F.B.I. and Homeland Security. If they discovered their locations, they would have the advantage. Unless President Vil authorized the use of the military on U.S. soil, the only way they could sustain any losses would be from federal agents to attack each location one by one.

Their raids of the supply warehouses were all successful. Colonel Inouye assessed that altogether they procured a three-year supply of MRE's with the current size of their forces. This was substantially more food rations than they would need, but the colonel addressed two issues; first, the food was not equally distributed among the forces; second, he wanted them to be conservative with the rations in case their numbers grew or Vil did not quickly leave power, which would result in a prolonged standoff.

Jasmine continued to coordinate with General Hamilton to ensure a successful delivery of their shipments of firearms, ammunition, and armory to their sites. This allowed them to begin training their forces with their weapons as they moved forward with their plans. Ensuring that their resistance forces were fully armed and trained was their primary objective for now. The next phase of Operations Fire Storm was to occur in just a few days' time.

NAVAL ASSAULT

January 18th, 2021

The U.S.S. Franklin D. Roosevelt had been sailing in non-territorial waters about a hundred nautical miles off the coast of San Diego for a week. With the nation in crisis, Atticus knew that the west coast fleet would depart the naval bases as soon as they could fuel and stock the ships. It had been over a week and they still had not tracked any ships on radar depart the port. He began to worry that something of a larger scale was being planned.

He and his department heads ran through several possible scenarios of what they would encounter when they confront the ships as they leave port. They tested the scenarios with the remaining crew to rum through every possible outcome. They were just one guided missile destroyer and there were over seventy naval warships and three aircraft carriers that they would soon confront.

It was now just two days before the second inauguration ceremony for President Vil. It was early on that Monday morning when Atticus suddenly woke, hours before sunrise. He was covered in sweat and breathing frantically. He felt an urgency to have the ship move closer to the coast of San Diego. He called up to the bridge and ordered the officer of the deck to direct the ship due east to a position eight miles off the coast of the port city.

He had a gut feeling that the fleet would depart that morning, just as the inauguration week was about to begin. The ship arrived at the intended position just before 6 a.m., with sunrise almost an hour away. He ordered the launch of their helicopter to patrol the naval bases and evaluate whether the ships were preparing for sea.

The helicopter crew flew over the naval bases to discover all the evidentiary signs of ships preparing for sea. Several ships were already being assisted into the harbor by tugboats, with numerous others casting off their lines from shore, while the rest were in the final stages of disconnecting their shore power lines. The pilot radioed back to the ship to inform them that it appeared the entire fleet was in the process of heading out to sea.

"Sir, if the first ship is just now approaching the Coronado Bay Bridge, then we have less than forty-five minutes before they clear the channel and make it to open ocean," stated the ship's navigator.

"Very well then, sound the alarm for general quarters, we need the crew at their battlestations. Call the department heads to the bridge. We have a new scenario confronting us, one that we should have considered from the beginning."

Atticus had prepared his crew for several small-scale battle engagements where they would have the upper hand. They had a fully inventoried armory and the crew had undergone a week straight of back-to-back drills in preparation for that scenario. He believed that the west coast fleet would depart in groups, but this new scenario with the entire fleet leaving port the same day forced Atticus to quickly adjust their plans. His new idea was the only option they had against a fleet of over seventy ships. The crew manned their battlestations in five minutes.

"Sir, all battle stations are manned. All department heads are present except the operations officer who is in the combat information center," announced the navigator.

"I will dial down to his direct line so he can understand what we are about to do," replied Atticus, dialing the phone directly to Lieutenant Birksby in the combat information center.

"Okay we have a quick decision to make. The entire fleet is getting underway, the first ship should be out of restricted waters in less than half an hour. I believe we have an opportunity here to disable the entire west coast fleet before they enter open ocean.

"We can launch a torpedo at the lead ship before it exits the channel to render it inoperable and cause it to run aground. The channel is very narrow so if we can block it then we render the entire fleet useless. This option will also limit the loss to life, which I know we all want to keep to a minimum."

"Sir, what if the ship is able to maneuver to avoid blocking the channel?" asked the combat systems officer.

"Then we launch additional torpedoes at the next ship or until we block the channel. They are in restricted waters, so they won't be able to maneuver to avoid the torpedoes."

"Our best chance to force a ship aground and block the channel is to hit them as they approach Shelter Island going around the bend. By my assessment, we will have to launch in about ten minutes in order to pull this off," stated the navigator.

"Any reason to not go forward?" Atticus asked the department heads.

"No," they replied in succession.

"There is no turning back now," Atticus stated, "Prepare the torpedoes for launch."

The ship made the approach closer to the bay entrance as they observed the lead ship, an old Ticonderoga class cruiser, approach the bend at Shelter Island. The combat systems officer notified the bridge that the torpedoes tubes were ready for launch. Atticus took in a deep breath.

"Fire two torpedoes!" he ordered.

"Roger, sir, firing two torpedoes!" exclaimed the combat systems officer.

Atticus heard the torpedoes launch. He walked out to the starboard bridge wing to get a better look. The bridge crew looked on in suspense. Just over a week ago they would never have envisioned attacking another U.S. naval warship. Today, they were about to witness the sinking of one.

They watched the torpedo trails as they entered the channel. In the distance, they could hear the collision alarm being activated on the Ticonderoga class cruiser. Within a few seconds, they no longer saw the trail. Atticus peered into his binoculars for a closer look.

He watched the explosion as the first torpedo struck the port side of the ship. Within a few seconds the sound of the explosion reached the U.S.S. Franklin D. Roosevelt, forcing everyone topside to cover their ears as the noise rolled over the ship. Before Atticus had a chance to accept what had just occurred, the navigator placed his hand on his shoulder.

"Sir, it appears the second torpedo was also a direct hit; port side."

They looked on in disbelief, taking in the ramifications of their actions. Atticus had just launched a successful unprovoked attack on another U.S. naval warship.

The ship began to slow, drifting slowly to its port side. It appeared from their point of view that the ship was taking on water as it appeared to be sinking slowly. The ship finally stopped moving, appearing to have run aground.

The navigator looked at the charts and radar to assess the ship's exact location in relation to the channel. He had bad news to report.

"Sir, it appears that the ship was able to successful navigate clear of the channel."

"That was my greatest worry," he replied. He looked up, pointing his index finger in the direction of the bay. He was directing the navigator's attention toward the next ship, it was an aircraft carrier. It appeared to be continuing along the channel route.

"Why are they still proceeding through the channel?"

"It looks as if they might be slowing, maybe to ensure they do not hit the cruiser as they pass by. They cannot just turn around in the bay so they must either continue, do a full stop, or full reverse. Load another round of torpedoes. We have to block the channel."

Within moments the next set of torpedoes were loaded. Atticus gave the order to fire two more torpedoes. They looked on in dreadful anticipation, watching the torpedoes as they entered the channel.

The aircraft carrier appeared to be rapidly slowing as the two torpedoes approached. The collision alarm was now audible in the distance. There was no ability to maneuver that large of a vessel in the narrow channel.

Boom! A cloud of smoke appeared from the stern of the aircraft carrier.

"It was a direct hit!" the navigator exclaimed. "What about the second torpedo?"

They continued to look on, waiting for the second torpedo to strike. After about thirty seconds, they realized the second torpedo must have missed. The aircraft carrier was no longer moving. It would be awhile before they could assess whether they had blocked the channel from any naval ships being able to pass through. For now, it appeared that the entire fleet had halted their movement in the bay. The ships that were closest to the base appeared to be returning pier side.

"Sir, sir, we have a problem. Look!"

The navigator pointed in the direction of the aircraft carrier. Two helicopters were lifting off from the flight deck of the aircraft carrier headed in their direction.

"It gets worse. There seems to be movement from the runway at the naval air station. I see jets moving onto the runway!" shouted the lookout in the bridge wing.

"I guess we won't be sticking around to make a battle damage assessment. Officer of the deck, have the combat information center direct the gunner's mates to position the 5-inch gun mount in the direction of the runway. I want the gunners to fire every round they have until that runway no longer exists. Navigator, get our helo to intercept those incoming helicopters and slow them down. Chief engineer, once we bombard that runway, I want us making flank speed westward. We need to put as much distance between us and the shore as possible."

The gunner's mates quickly prepared the 5-inch gun mount to fire on the runway. Within moments the gun was ready to fire. The ship's helo was still in the air and headed on a course to intercept the incoming helicopters.

"The 5-inch gun is ready, sir. Would you like to order weapons release?" asked the officer of the deck.

"Commence continuous fire on target!"

Boom!...Boom!...Boom!

The shots continued uninterrupted for several minutes. At the same time they unloaded on the runway, their helo successfully engaged on one of the incoming helicopters.

It launched a barrage of gunfire on it, causing it to fall into a tailspin and rapid descent toward the ocean surface. The second helicopter conducted an effective evasion maneuver and continued toward the ship.

As the helicopter made its approach, Atticus knew he had one final response to stop them before they reached the ship. He ordered the tactical action officer to fire the Phalanx close-in weapon system (CIWS) directly at the helicopter. The rapid-fire gun would be capable of unleashing over 4,500 rounds a minute on the helicopter. It was a last resort, but one that would eliminate the threat.

"Unleash the Phalanx CIWS on the helicopter!"

The command was met with an immediate onslaught of rapid gunfire from the aft CIWS gun mount firing toward the ship's port side. Atticus looked on from the bridge to see what could only be described as a laser beam in the direction of the helicopter. He looked on as the rounds met their target and destroyed the helicopter.

"Cease fire, cease fire, all mounts!"

Atticus and the officer of the deck walked out onto the bridge wing to assess the damage the 5-inch gun had done to the runway. They both looked through their binoculars to determine if the barrage on the runway rendered it useless.

"Sir, it appears that the jets are not moving on the runway. I think we put enough holes in that runway for the time being."

"I believe you are right. But that only bought us a little bit of time. Set the ship on a course west bound at flank speed. Give the chief engineer any support he needs to make it happen. We need to get away from the shoreline as quickly as possible and reduce their ability to track us."

CHAPTER 6

THE PUPPET MASTER

VOW TO ANNIHILATE THE TERROSISTS

January 19th, 2021

W ord of the naval attack on the Pacific Fleet was slow to reach the nation. Power was still out in most cities, suburban communities, and rural areas. Some of the largest cities were finally receiving intermittent but unreliable power with outages occurring several times a day. The resistance force hackers were still constantly attacking the power grids to keep the nation in the dark before the next phase was complete.

By the time word of the attack reached the White House, President Vil was putting the finishing touches on the speech he would deliver the next day at his second inaugural ceremony. He planned to give a radical address to the nation and to the world where he would promise to eradicate anyone that is defiant of his reign of power. The elimination of any opposition to him was all that consumed his daily agenda. This attack just dealt him a major blow that would require an immediate response.

"Father, the Pacific Fleet came under attack yesterday. There was a rogue ship, the U.S.S. Franklin D. Roosevelt, that attacked one of our aircraft carriers and a cruiser in the San Diego harbor as the fleet was heading to sea. The two ships ran aground and blocked the rest of the fleet from being able to get out of the harbor. They also took out the runway at the naval air station on Coronado Island.

"Marine fighters out of Miramar Air Station were dispatched to locate and destroy the ship, but so far they have been unsuccessful in locating the ship. Ships out of Washington and Hawaii have gone to sea to find and destroy the rogue ship," Sophia Kaiser informed her father, whom had now been sworn in as Vice President, and his most loyal advisor.

"No, this cannot be happening! Right before I am to give a speech to the nation that will affirm my right to rule over this land for a generation! Once word of this reaches the people it will make me look weak. These rebels are traitors to their nation. I want to immediately brand them as terrorists and use our military to weed them out!" exclaimed President Vil.

"Well we have the remaining ships in the Pacific out looking for the rogue ship. We are confident that they will find the ship within a few days time. When you are ready to give the order to use the military on the rebels then we can root them out of their bunkers and stop any more planned attacks they have before they can follow through."

"Yes, it is time we call on the powers granted to me in the Insurrection Act to respond to these acts of terror. We will not look weak in front of the patriotic Americans that support us. We must keep them on our side, especially now that we are on the verge of becoming leaders for life. Things are just too unstable to show any form of weakness right now."

"We must first ensure that tomorrow's ceremonies are safe. They must go off without any issues, especially since President Porchensky of Russia will be here. He is due to arrive today, am I right father?"

"Yes, he will be here this afternoon. I forgot to mention it before, but we will have dinner with him this evening; a pre-celebratory dinner. I want you there to meet him, he is a superb leader, one that you will come to admire."

"Not as much as I admire you father. You are the greatest leader the world has ever known!"

"Of course! But he is the reason that we are here…in power…ruling over this nation…making ourselves rich off of it…while leaving this nation to fall apart ever so slowly and end up in the ash heap of history."

"We have taken advantage of the American people our entire lives and played them for fools. Now we finally have the power to rule over these people by making them fear the unknown world without you to safeguard them," Sophia asserted.

"Oh, how you charm me with your words. Go and give the orders to mobilize the military and have them weed out these terrorists. We must quickly end their attempts to delegitimize my right to reign over this nation!"

"Yes father, I will take care of that now before we have dinner with President Porchensky. What time would you like for Jerry and I to come over for dinner?"

"I want you both here before 6:30 p.m. for the social hour. I would like for us to give him a great first impression of the White House, this will be his first time here. He should arrive shortly after 6:30 p.m."

"Well, you can expect us to be in our very best dinner attire. Is Melanie going to be accompanying you?"

"Yes, I expect her to at least stick around through dinner. You know she does not like the spotlight so I am sure that she will retire upstairs to the residence before dessert."

"I expect that is when you will want to talk about the future alliance between our nations?"

"Of course. There will be too many of the staff around during the social hour and dinner. We will save our plans until the end of the night when we have some privacy and can be free to discuss our future endeavors."

Sophia left to the Pentagon to discuss military plans with her husband, the newly appointed Secretary of Defense. Meanwhile, President Vil continued refining his speech for the inauguration ceremony. He wanted to add wordage about 'law and order' to show that he was in command and should be feared.

THE SOURCE OF D.E.VIL'S POWER

Russian President Vladimir Porchensky landed in Washington, D.C. late in the afternoon, the day before President Vil was to be sworn back in as President of the United States for a second term. Unbeknownst to anyone else, it would be the second and final term. President Vil was about to unveil his plan to suspend further presidential elections during the ongoing chaos and request emergency powers to remain in office indefinitely. He had control of both chambers of Congress after he had all the Democrats arrested; so his request would be carried out into law. Then, after being granted the powers of unlimited rule, he would sideline the Congress as an inconsequential and incompetent body.

Just as planned, all of President Vil's family had arrived early to greet the Russian president for his arrival at the White House. His wife and children were to attend the social hour and dinner but leave the two presidents and Sophia to discuss the pressing matters ahead of them in private afterward. The Vil family only knew that the two men had business dealings together. Sophia, however, knew about their family's Russian heritage and KGB connection.

When President Porchensky arrived, he was greeted first by President Vil and his wife Melanie, followed by each of their children. The children were quick to fight for the attention of the Russian leader, each of them nudging their way in to shake his hand and introduce themselves. Their eagerness annoyed their father. He quickly beckoned for everyone to head inside the White House for the Blue Room.

"President Vil, this is such an exquisite building. I imagine you enjoy calling this place home, yes?" President Porchensky inquired.

"I actually prefer the penthouse in my high-rise tower in Manhattan over this old home. This place needs a facelift. I tried to get them to redo the interior in gold, but several politicians told me that it would be met with backlash by the people. I still do not agree with them and maybe soon we will make it happen."

"That is not something you will need to worry about for much longer as you will soon have powers greater than you ever imagined."

"Yes, I may finally get the chance to turn this place gold. It should by suitable for a king and kings love gold!"

"What are you going to do about these terrorists that have taken out your Pacific Fleet and have amassed a significant number of recruits to join their ranks?" Porchensky asked. "Someone who wants to have the power of a king would not let this stand."

"I will address that issue tomorrow during my inaugural address. Please let us enjoy some cocktails and dinner first. Then we can discuss our plans after we have enjoyed this amazing meal that my chef has prepared for us."

The two men discussed routine matters of politics while enjoying champagne and hors d'oeuvres. Vil's children continuously vying for time with the Russian president kept interrupting them. When dinner was ready, the group headed down the hall into the State Dining Room. They were greeted with an elegant table display, fitting for a foreign head of state. President Vil sat at the head of the table, with his wife Melanie at his right, and President Porchensky to his left. Sophia and her husband Jerry sat next to the Russian leader, while the rest of Vil's children filled the remaining spots at the table.

During the dinner, the conversation revolved around questions the family had about Russia. Don Jr., the president's eldest child, inquired about the prospects of opening a tall condominium complex in Moscow. President Porchensky, eloquently dismissed the inquiry by asking the eldest son to make a proposal and the men could speak at a later date about it, knowing all too well that he would never again see Vil's children.

After dinner, the family left the dining room, led by Melanie. Only the two presidents and Sophia remained. This was their opportunity to discuss their private plans. However, President Vil had other questions he wanted answered. These were questions that his parents never answered when he was a young man and aspiring businessman. He had the very man that ordered his family sent to the United States decades ago to be spies for Russia right in front of him. Donald recommended the three go to into the Red Room to continue their discussions in private.

"So Vladimir, we have had the great fortune of meeting on a few occasions, however, we have not had the opportunity to have any conversation in private, except over the phone."

"I believe you are right. Well, now we can finally talk about our plans for this nation you rule over."

"Yes, yes, but let us save those conversations for tomorrow after the inauguration. I would like to talk about my parents right now. As you know, they did not tell me much about their lives before they came to this country. I was educated to become successful in order to take over the family business from them when they passed on. We have funneled massive fortunes of money through our real estate empire on behalf of the Russian Federation. We have built gorgeous buildings all over this country to reward Russian oligarchs with luxurious properties.

"But all that my parents ever told me about our history is that we came here when I was an infant and that I was to take over the family business. They told me that if I was ever asked about my birthplace, I was to tell them that my mother gave birth to me at home with the aid of a midwife. They trained me to be an American by birth but a Russian by loyalty. I was to remain loyal to the motherland and then I would learn of my mission when the time was ready."

"It seems that you already know so much. What else is it that you want to know?"

"How did they get involved in the KGB? What did they do? Why were they brought over? Why was my birth certificate forged to make me an American citizen?"

"Is that all?" asked Porchensky.

"No, not even close. But I think it is a good start."

"Where do I start? Let me think. Your parents were both close to Joseph Stalin. When he became the Premier of the Soviet Union, he entrusted them with certain responsibilities that could not be officially carried out by the government. They were very good at what they did. You can consider what they were able to accomplish as the predecessor to what eventually became known as the KGB.

"Your mother got pregnant near the end of World War Two. She had made a vow to not have children due to her very specific skillset as an assassin and assassins are not meant to be mothers. Stalin would have eliminated her from the role she played in his secret agency had he known. She did the best to hide her pregnancy, but when word made it back to Stalin that she had betrayed her oath, he was furious.

"He was going to have her killed but your father begged for mercy. He committed to anything that Stalin wanted if he did not order the execution of you and your mother. He was even willing to take a mission to Siberia. However, the war was near its end and Stalin believed he could use them elsewhere. He sent them to the United States to be spies.

"He had all three of you sent to New York City with false paperwork, including your doctored birth certificate, to await further orders. He had not committed to a specific mission for them, they were just told to start a new life in the United States. They were given plenty of money to get started while they waited to hear from Moscow.

"Shortly after they arrived, your father took some of the money and he bought an apartment complex. He quickly learned the New York City real estate world and built wealth through several real estate deals. Stalin continued to monitor your parents' success until his death. They never heard from him before he died.

"They were concerned after his death as they did not know whether they would ever receive orders or if anyone else knew of their mission. They did not know if Stalin had ever mentioned them to any of his loyal advisors. They continued to build their real estate empire. When the KGB was officially formed, I was one of the first agents to earn the trust and respect of Stalin's successor Nikita Khrushchev.

"He was one of the only advisors that Stalin had trusted with the knowledge of your parents. Khrushchev tasked me with conveying a message to your parents that they were to transform their real estate empire into a money laundering business for Russian oligarchs. I was just a young man, not too many years out of KGB training. I was intimidated by the history of what your parents accomplished during the 1930's and 40's.

"They were legends in the agency; first, with the industrialization and collectivization periods, then the purges, and finally during the Second World War. I flew to New York to deliver the message personally. I wanted to meet them and see what I could learn from them. I think you were almost a teenager at the time. I was in my early twenties and had only been an agent for a few years."

"Wait! We met when I was a child?" Vil asked.

"Yes, briefly. It was during my first trip to the United States. I met your father at one of his construction sites. We were in the middle of talking about the Soviet Union's intentions for them. You barged into the office after school that day. I remember you complaining about being bullied at school. Your father was very displeased with you interrupting us. He yelled at you to get out. As you stormed out, I stopped you and gave you some words of advice."

Remembering the words from several decades ago, Vil replied, "People who attack you physically or verbally and try to reduce your confidence and self-esteem are very aware of your potential, and you have a great deal of potential in you. They are just schoolyard bullies and they will go on to live empty, meaningless lives. You on the other hand will go on to do great things so long as you listen to your parents and learn from them."

"Yes, it appears that I was right. You learned from your parents and turned that potential into reality."

"Indeed, I did. So, what happened after you met with my parents?" Vil asked.

"They took the message from Khrushchev very well; I could tell that their loyalty was still to the motherland. We continued to relay messages to them over the years. I remained a liaison between Moscow and your parents. We had the understanding that one day they would give you more details of the family business and the connections back to Moscow.

"Your father relayed to us that he had begun to prepare you to take over the business operations. He had just started teaching you about how it functioned on behalf of the Soviet Union before his untimely death. When your parents died suddenly in that tragic car accident we did not know if you were ready to take over. When you reached out to us shortly after, the agency was not sure what to make of it. We did not know whether your loyalty was to the motherland or to the United States. I made the decision that we could trust you and continue our previous operations unimpeded.

"You did just that. For years you helped us make our oligarchs wealthier than they ever dreamed. You took the operation to a new level and in return you became even wealthier. After the Soviet Union's collapse, we pulled back. It was after my successful coup, when I became president, that I decided we would use you for something greater.

"I was not quite sure what that mission would be until I met your predecessor. He placed strong sanctions on our nation and froze the assets of our oligarchs. I decided that we would use your fame and wealth to our advantage. We would get you to run for President of the United States and help you win at all costs.

"When you came to Russia several years ago on a business trip you met with one of my oligarchs. He was one of my closest allies. He inquired about your desire to run for president on our behalf. You quickly shot him down because you were having too much fun living the luxurious life of a billionaire. So, we executed our back up plan on you.

"We sent some of our best Russian prostitutes to your hotel room that night as a 'gift' for all the wealth you had brought our oligarchs. What you did not know at the time was that your room was bugged with cameras. A year later we sent the footage to you with a note that encouraged you to highly reconsider the offer to run for president so that the footage would not make its way to the public. If there is anything you are insecure about it is about the image you want to portray in public.

"And now we are here. You beat your opponent, with our help in the cyber realm and through social media. It was our most successful psychological operations campaign we ever conducted. I guess forging an American birth certificate paid off. We originally just wanted to give you citizenship so that it would not bring attention to your family.

"We wanted to make you all appear as American as possible. They worked relentlessly to get rid of their accent. Those were tense times between our nations. What we ended up with was the best opportunity to destroy the United States…from within."

"I have so many more questions. Can we continue this conversation?"

"Of course, you can ask me as many questions as you would like," replied Porchensky.

"This is going to be a long night. Can you have the chefs bring out our dessert and some wine?" Vil asked, turning to his daughter Sophia.

The three leaders continued their conversation for several hours. They finally parted ways shortly after midnight, allowing them to have a few hours of rest before the inaugural ceremony the following day.

OPERATION FIRE STORM UNLEASHED

January 20th, 2021

BOOM!

The deafening explosion was so powerful it knocked President Vil out of his bed. His wife Melanie immediately jumped out from under the covers onto her feet.

Secret Service agents immediately swarmed the master bedroom, weapons drawn. They ran toward the president and his wife so they could remove them from the residence. One agent threw their robes at them and told them to put them on immediately.

"What is going on? What was that loud noise?" President Vil asked the agents.

They did not respond. There was no time to answer his questions. The explosion set into place their preset response to take the president to the PEOC; or as the agents referred to it, the bunker. One group of agents circled the president, another his wife. They grabbed them by their sleepwear and forced them out of the bedroom, into the hallway where they could eliminate any potential threat from the outside.

Proceeding down the main stairway, they were met with several more agents. Once they reached the main level they proceeded for the stairwell that would take them down to the PEOC.

BOOM! BOOM! BOOM! BOOM! BOOM! BOOM!

The explosions continued! This time multiple explosions more deafening than the first! Everyone was knocked to the ground.

"We need to secure the president! We must get him to the bunker immediately!" exclaimed one of the agents.

"No, the explosions are too close! We need to get him and his wife out of the White House! Take them into the tunnels! We will exit south to the monument!" exclaimed another agent, appearing to be in charge of the detail.

The agents picked the president up, surrounding him, then pushed him through the corridor, down a flight of stairs, into a kitchen, and then a dark hallway; his wife in tow. They emerged at a dead end, where an agent entered a code into a panel, unlocking a thick metal door. They continued through the corridor, stopping only to survey any obstacles in front of them.

BOOM! BOOM! BOOM! BOOM! BOOM! BOOM!
BOOM! BOOM! BOOM! BOOM! BOOM! BOOM!
BOOM! BOOM! BOOM! BOOM! BOOM! BOOM!

This time the earth was shaken so much, that the concrete walls that surrounded them; far, far beneath the surface began to crack!

"Let's go! We need to move now! Just grab them and move forward! There is no time! Stagecoach is waiting for us at the rendezvous!" the agent exclaimed, referring to the presidential motorcade.

The agents again grabbed the president and his wife, both of which were still completely clueless to what was happening. They arrived at the rendezvous point, several floors below the surface.

"I'll go up first and check for Stagecoach!" You guys wait here!" the lead agent ordered.

BOOM! BOOM! BOOM! BOOM! BOOM! BOOM!
BOOM! BOOM! BOOM! BOOM! BOOM! BOOM!
BOOM! BOOM! BOOM! BOOM! BOOM! BOOM!

A fourth barrage of explosions roared overhead.

"Nevermind, we do not have time! Let's get to the surface! We have to get them out of here!"

Quickly, they darted up the stairs, arriving at an inside entrance to the Washington Monument. Things had become very hazy after all the explosions. President Vil began to panic as the small, confined space closed in on him. He started gasping for air.

"We need to get to the surface! I don't care if the motorcade is out there or not, I cannot breathe down here!" Vil exclaimed.

The lead agent entered a code, opening another metal door, exposing them to fresh air. They were still two flights below the surface, but they continued up the stairwell. When they reached the exit, the agent looked back at the group.

He shouted, "I'll go first, when I give the all clear, bring the president and his wife out, surrounding them until we get to the rendezvous point."

The agent shoved the door open and blasted through the exit while the president, his wife, and the other agents waited inside. He quickly returned after assessing the scene.

"Sir, we've got to get you out of here. The motorcade is coming up the road and will be here in less than a minute. I need to warn you, when we step outside you will not like what you see," he stated while gesturing to the agents to surround the president and his wife.

They emerged at the surface where they observed a night sky transformed into daylight. It was lit up by a fiery red light in all directions. The president ordered the agents to stop, to get a better look at the destruction. He peered far down the National Mall in the direction of the Capitol building. It was no longer recognizable as a building. Fires engulfed the remains of the former building.

The president stood frozen in disbelief. The capitol region was under siege. Destruction consumed everything around him. An attempted coup to sabotage his official reinstatement as president was underway and there was nothing he could do in that moment to stop it.

The sound of police, fire, and ambulance sirens zooming past, brought him back to reality. He turned to assess the damage of the other buildings. It was hard for him to determine exactly which ones had been attacked. He saw flames had engulfed several buildings in the direction of the F.B.I. and Justice Department headquarters. One of the agents gasped, getting the attention of the president. He turned to look in the direction of the agent.

What caught his attention though, was the massive fires and explosions across the Potomac River. The Pentagon was ablaze. Massive plumes of smoke could be seen in the red sky over the Pentagon. As the president stared at the building as it became engulfed in flames, he heard a swooshing sound overhead. He looked up and saw several objects speeding over his head.

BOOM! BOOM! BOOM!

The president dropped to the ground to take cover. Three agents ran in his direction to surround him. After several seconds, the explosions ceased, and the president was assisted onto his feet by the agents. The motorcade had finally arrived. The agents dragged the president to the motorcade, shoving him and his wife into the backseat.

The tires screeched as the motorcade fled the scene. The president finally secure in his seat, peeked out the window. He was still in disbelief that an attack on the homeland was occurring before his very eyes. He looked to see where the latest explosion had landed.

"Where did that last set of explosions hit?" he asked. He hoped that someone in the car noticed where the latest round of missiles landed.

The agent in the front passenger seat pointed toward the decimated building, "Mr. President, it looks like they have taken out the White House."

As they rounded the corner, the destruction became visible to President Vil. The White House had just been hit, along with the Eisenhower Executive Office Building that sat adjacent to the White House. It appeared that the entire complex was destroyed. It was hard for him to make any real assessment as the night's illuminated sky was blocked out by smoke and ash. As the president scanned outside of the vehicle all he could make out was dark outlines of buildings surrounded by smoke and a light colorful white and red glow in all directions.

The president's motorcade quickly fled the scene. With communications now down and no means of aerial extraction, the agents decided to take the president to Joint Base Andrews. They determined that they could regroup there and provide the president with the protection of a military base with thousands of troops and several undeclared bunkers to provide underground cover.

A NOT-SO-PRESIDENTIAL INAUGURATION

The presidential motorcade arrived safely at Joint Base Andrews where the president and his wife were taken to an undisclosed bunker. The president, now safe in the bunker, turned his attention to the unknown status of the Russian president and his own daughter, his vice president. After yelling at his Secret Service agents and constantly asking for updates, they informed to him that all forms of communication remained down. They had no idea when communications would be restored.

The president furiously paced back and forth for hours. He wanted to know if his daughter made it out safely. He was also worried about an international crisis with the Russian president on U.S. soil during an attack. After all, Vladimir Porchensky was his mentor.

The president, unable to sleep after the attack and due to the unknown whereabouts of his daughter and the Russian leader, requested his Secret Service detail take him outside to survey the damage. They cautioned him to stay below ground for security reasons, but they also knew there was limited ability to assess damage from several miles away. The agents ultimately acquiesced and went above ground, ahead of the president, to secure the area.

When the president arrived at the surface, shortly after sunrise, he witnessed the destruction from the outskirts of the city. The damage from the attack had blanketed the sky in a sea of smoke. Sirens could be heard in the distance, along with the occasional sound of helicopters and military jets flying overhead.

After several minutes, an agent approached the president. He whispered in his ear to inform him that communications in the bunker had been restored. They were able to contact his daughter Sophia and she was waiting to speak with him. He immediately ran back down into the bunker to talk with his daughter.

"Sophia! Sophia! Are you alright? Where did they take you?"

"Yes, we are safe now at the Marine Corps Base at Quantico Station. Shortly after the attack started, our Secret Service detail nabbed us out of our residence and proceeded to take us to the Pentagon where they assured us that we would be safe. We had almost arrived when we saw the explosions. It was horrible daddy!

"They decided that we should flee the city, so they brought us to Quantico. So far things have been quiet down here. How are things where you are at? Are you safe?"

"Melanie and I are safe in a bunker at Joint Base Andrews. Have you heard anything? Do you know what has happened with President Porchensky?"

"Yes, we have had some contact with other agents down here. It appears that they have taken out the F.B.I and Justice Department headquarters along with the Capitol Building and White House. The N.S.A. and C.I.A. headquarters were taken out too. We believe they also took out some of the nation's federal strategic sites. There are some unconfirmed reports that some bases were targeted and may have come under attack, but nothing has been confirmed as of yet.

"We believe President Porchensky's security detail got him out of the White House. I have some agents looking into it and another set of agents headed to Reagan International Airport, where his plane was waiting. If he made it out safe, then we will know once the agents get there. I will let you know immediately once we get a status update."

"I cannot believe these terrorists. The have ruined my big day! I had such an epic speech to give to the people today. Believe me, it was going to be one of my best speeches! Probably the best speech in all of history!"

"Oh father, you always give the best speeches. Your followers love the red meat you throw them when you call your political enemies derogatory names. I am sure that you would have given such a great speech that the people would be calling for you to stay in power forever."

"This speech was going to be my best one by far. I was planning to call for an end to the congress and to the courts. I am tired of them being a roadblock to my agenda. They move so slow and prevent me from getting my way. It will be so much easier to get things done without them. It is time that we consolidate power under a Vil dynasty!"

"That is okay father, you will have your chance to give an epic speech soon enough. Maybe it is for the best anyway. Most of the nation is still without power and cell phone service is intermittent. Hardly anyone would have been witness to your speech in real time. You will not have the ability to reach most Americans until we can restore power, cell phone service, and social media."

"You are right, this will give me more time to prepare an even bolder speech. Now I can include a demand to mobilize my followers to attack these terrorists!"

Several hours went by with no word about the fate of President Porchensky. A furious Donald Vil demanded to leave the safety and security of the base to get a tour of the destruction from the above. The Secret Service scrambled to coordinate the arrival of the presidential helicopter, known as Marine One, to take the president on an aerial tour to survey the destruction.

Late in the afternoon, the president finally got his wish. Marine One, along with several helicopter escorts, took the president around Washington, D.C. What they saw was the total annihilation of federal government buildings, including the Capitol Building and the White House. The only government buildings that the president could identify as still standing were the museums along the National Mall and the memorials for Abraham Lincoln, Thomas Jefferson, Franklin D. Roosevelt, and Martin Luther King, Jr. The Washington Memorial had partially collapsed, the top half of the structure now lay at the base of what remained.

It was clear to the president now that the resistance movement was not just a fringe element of terrorists. They are a well-organized group hell bent on removing him from power at any cost. He was now determined to unleash the full furry of the U.S. military forces on anyone that stands in the way of Villain power. He was prepared to issue the order to unleash the power of the military on any American that stands in the way of his agenda immediately upon his return to the base.

Just as Donald Vil's presidential helicopter landed back at the base, he was alerted to an incoming transmission from the Russian president. He quickly proceeded to the bunker to hear the message from his mentor. He hoped for a message that was uplifting because he felt so lost and in need of direction.

"Dominik, if you receive this message then you made it out alive before your beautiful capitol was destroyed. I made it out safely just as the missiles were coming down on the city. My intelligence forces were not prepared for this sudden and massive attack.

"It seems as if we have both underestimated who or what we are dealing with. You must get a grip on this issue and do it quickly. Whatever force we are now dealing with is better at operational security than I would have ever assumed Americans could manage. We were both caught off-guard by these terrorists.

"You must destroy the enemy before they get the upper hand. Americans are swayed by public opinion more than any other society I have known. If they are able to convey that they are in control and that they know how to defeat you then you may not have the support of the public. You may even lose the support of your most ardent supporters. You must commence a massive strike against these forces, immediately.

"We will provide you with intelligence and surveillance support. It is now in your hands to sew chaos on the American people. This is the one chance in our lifetime to make Russia great again! I am counting on you to deliver this final blow to American dominance so that I can make Russia the dominant force in the world!"

Donald Vil hung up the phone. The message was clear, he must seek revenge for this attack on his rule. He must hunt down anyone that defied his rule and eliminate the resistance. It was time for him to unleash his wrath!

NOT-SO-CEREMONIAL INAUGURATION

Late in the evening, the Chief Justice of the Supreme Court arrived at the base. He was escorted under the protection of a heavy security detail. He was taken into the bunker, where he was to swear in Donald Vil to a second term as president. He believed that he must be sworn in on that day. After the attacks that had just occurred, he felt the people would give him a mandate to do almost anything to protect them as he saw fit.

He had intended to give a major speech at his second inauguration that day. He had planned to declare triumph over his political enemies, declare himself so popular to the American people that he should be installed as president for life, and he would declare the Legislative Branch no longer relevant, and call for the American people to rise up and help him remove anyone that stood in his way.

His grandiose plan, however, never unfolded as he envisioned. He was now hiding in a bunker with the hope that his location would not be discovered by whomever clearly wanted him removed from power. What was meant to be a moment in front of the nation and the world, was now a small ceremony with only the Chief Justice of the Supreme Court, a few of his loyal aids, and his security detail. His self-congratulatory speech would have to wait for another day.

"Mr. President, are you ready?" asked the Chief Justice.

"Yes, let us begin," replied the disheartened Vil.

"Alright, Mr. President, repeat after me….."

CHAPTER 7

RISE OF THE RESISTANCE

RESISTANCE HEADQUARTERS

January 25th, 2021

I t had been five intensely long days since the full force of Operation Fire Storm had gone into effect. Several hours had passed since the first wave of the attack before the resistance forces could assess the damage they caused to federal facilities and several strategic military installations. Almost every site that they targeted in the operation had successfully been destroyed. Only a few missiles did not hit their intended target. A handful of those missiles ended up hitting residential or commercial buildings. They knew that hundreds of innocent lives would be lost from the attacks. The leadership believed that they had no other choice than to strike first in order to gain a strategic advantage against Vil.

Rosa Perez had given the order for the attack during the middle of the night to minimize the loss of life and casualties. Conrad's team had run numerous scenarios so they could achieve a favorable outcome from a strategic perspective. No matter the scenario, the inevitable result included deaths of government employees, military officials, and innocent nearby civilians. They were also aware of the likely possibility that some missiles would miss their intended target, causing unknown loss of life scenarios. No matter the ultimate outcome, their best scenario had been to attack during the middle of the night, hours before the inauguration ceremony. The mission, although not flawless, appeared to have been a success.

During their initial planning phase of the operation, one of the additions to Conrad's team, an employee of a major Silicon Valley technology company, proved his expertise as a superior hacker. He had compromised several government systems. He was even able to successfully hack through the firewall in the government's missile launch system. When they discovered this vulnerability, they debated whether to materialize this into their operation.

After Conrad obtained approval from Rosa Perez, he allowed the hacker to install an encrypted virus that would deliver a payload when accessed by Conrad. The payload in this case, was the coordinates for the sites that they needed to destroy. This would give them the advantage against better equipped forces. The launch was to commence once Conrad selected the date. They finally chose the night before the inauguration. Conrad had the launch times uploaded into the malware.

They monitored the mission from a geosynchronous satellite they had seized control of in space. The heat sensor activity on the surface showed that the missile launches from numerous missile silos from secret government locations in the heartland of the nation had indeed impacted their targets. Conrad could only imagine what went through the minds of the missile operators once they lost control of their missile launch systems and the missiles began their launch sequence. He also mourned the loss of innocent lives, although a known collateral of warfare, he felt nothing but sadness in his heart for those that paid the ultimate sacrifice.

The days following the operation, the destruction had disabled much of Vil's ability to launch a swift counterattack offensive. The power grid and communications networks remained largely offline with unreliable service in some areas. Although their mission had been successful, they no longer had access to the missile systems, a flaw they could only have encountered once. They believed the government's security systems were quickly upgraded in response to the missile attack to prevent further intrusion.

Conrad believed that the energy consumption levels that they were using at the headquarters might soon draw attention to their secret base in the Sierra Nevada mountains. They had increased their energy consumption from emergency generators, which create a heat signature that can be tracked. He also worried that the innocent lives lost in the first attack and the level of destruction they had done to major American institutions would compel some Americans to join their forces, but another group of Americans to join Vil's forces. Some would view what they had done as a first attack on the nation, while others could argue that the stealing of the election was the first attack.

He tasked his friend Jasmine with the extraordinary task of locating several alternative headquarters locations. They would need several locations for every regional headquarters since they were splintered throughout the country. Each headquarters would need the ability to take control of another region if they became compromised. They had a limited amount of time before major military operations would go into effect.

"Rosa, our team of hackers are not having any success getting back into the government servers. I think we will have to scrap our second wave of cyber warfare attacks and proceed with the plan without the cyber advantage," explained Conrad.

"Well, we were not optimistic that we would have a chance to conduct a second wave. We may not need that second wave. It looks like the momentum is moving to our side now," Rosa replied.

"I'm sorry, but I must not be up to speed. Our team has been so busy these last few days I have not been able to keep up with anything outside of this compound. What has changed?"

"To start, it looks like we have sent an effective message to the American people by striking first. We have shown that Vil and his evil henchmen are weak. They cannot even protect the government institutions from a bunch of…as he puts it…'disorganized thugs and terrorists.' We have been receiving reports that people are fed up with the lies and ready to start fresh with a new government.

"Our ranks our rapidly growing. The cities have become shells of what were once bustling cities. Millions of Americans have now joined up with us. Over the last few days our numbers have more than quadrupled and they are continuing to grow. The volunteer forces have also contributed greatly to the cause, providing us with weapons, munitions, electronics, surveillance technology, along with food and water. We have already begun moving our forces and attacking where we know we have the advantage.

"Unfortunately, with the good also comes the bad. Reports have come in that many Americans have fled to join Vil's forces. They have drawn a line in the sand and will remain loyal to him no matter what. This is just as we feared. The American people are as divided today as they were during our Civil War. We will not be able to avoid conflict and loss of life. This will be a battle for the soul of our nation. Good must prevail over evil or this will be the end of American democracy."

Conrad, feeling optimistic about the future, replied, "There is something that we have on our side that Vil will never have that gives us the advantage."

"And what is that?" Rosa asked.

"We have history on our side. In the course of human events, good may have not always triumphed over evil, but when good is threatened by evil, citizens become engaged and stand up against the threat of tyranny. There will be some that choose to fight on the wrong side of history, knowingly or not. They too will eventually come to see the light and accept the fate of righteousness, or they will become victim to the darkness.

"Their numbers are strong, and their capabilities outweigh our own. They have the power of the greatest military on the planet on their side. But I truly believe that we have history on our side. We are fighting for our freedom to live in a free world, one that is governed by laws and democratic principles. That is more powerful a message than that of pledging loyalty to a tyrant and fighting for an unjust cause over his endless lies and his betrayal of our Constitution."

"Wait, what did you say about what we are fighting for?" Rosa asked.

"We are fighting for our freedom. A freedom to live in a free world that is governed by laws and democratic principles."

"We have been sending the wrong message this entire time. Since the beginning of this we have coined the phrase 'resistance forces' as if we are resisting Vil and tyranny. We are not resisting him, we are fighting for our freedom. We are fighting for democracy," Rosa stated while pacing back and forth appearing to be in deep thought.

"Of course we are. That is what this is all about. We are fighting to free our country and return to a democratic society."

"Yes, but that has not been how we have constructed our message. Our message has been that of resistance. We need to shift that narrative into that of freedom. We are no longer 'the resistance,' we will now be known as the Freedom Forces!"

Conrad relished the idea of them being known as the Freedom Force. He already felt compelled to get the idea out to everyone before days end, but before he could even interject and convey the urgent need to shift their message, they were both interrupted by General Hamilton barging in on them.

"You both need to come out here to the command center. We have an emergency!" the general ordered.

They followed him out to a hectic command center. Everyone appeared to be packing things up and preparing to evacuate.

"It appears that Vil's forces have located us and have sent a team of B-2 bombers to take us out. They are coming from Whiteman Air Force Base so they could be armed with a nuclear arsenal. We need to evacuate immediately," declared General Hamilton.

"Are we sure that they are headed to our location?" Conrad asked.

"Yes, one of our sources on the ground outside the base intercepted a transmission as they were taking off. They were ordered to 'take out the enemy stronghold.' Our radar intercept has them headed directly to our location. We have no reason to believe they have not triangulated our location."

"We are deep underground. How could they have located us?" asked Rosa.

"This was actually one of my major concerns. We have been utilizing a massive power consumption to keep our systems online. As long as the power grids were down, I believed the threat to be minimal because they could not track our heat signature. We had a contingency plan to relocate in the works. It seems as though we should have sped that process up," answered Conrad.

"Yes, and now we have to vacate our main communications station with no back up plan. How will we coordinate the next attack? We are to execute our next phase in just over forty-eight hours from now!" she exclaimed.

"Then you will need to get word to our Freedom Forces that they are on their own. If General Hamilton concurs, I recommend we carry out the mission as planned. Our forces know what to do, they will just not have coordination from us. This will take us back to a pre-technology era, and we will have a harder mountain to climb, but we have to execute this mission if we want any chance of taking our nation back," stated Conrad.

"I concur with Conrad. Our regional commanders know what to do and are prepared to carry out this attack. If we cause any delay then we risk any advantage we may have. We have known all along that if this drags on for weeks or months then we will lose our advantage and quite possibly any potential to remove Vil from power. We must relocate now, and our forces must strike as planned," General Hamilton insisted.

Rosa agreed and quickly conveyed a message to the new Freedom Forces via encrypted message.

"To my fellow Freedom Forces, when you receive this message, you will be on your own. Our headquarters has been compromised. Continue your mission as planned. We must not allow any setback to stop us from securing freedom and democracy for our nation. If you do not hear from me within ninety-six hours, consider me gone. Governor Andrews of Colorado is now in charge of our Freedom Forces. May you all be blessed with the spirit of America, for she is not merely a place, but an idea that must live in our hearts and that we must be willing to fight for with our lives."

They packed up what remaining items they could take with them in the short time they had left and fled the headquarters. They split into several groups to reduce their chances of being tracked by Vil's forces. They were on their own now.

NEW LEADERSHIP

January 28th, 2021

Soon after their commander's message was conveyed, word of a massive plume of smoke that blanketed the upper Sierra Nevada mountains began to circulate the remaining radio waves. Their headquarters had been compromised. Their senior leaders were missing. They were on their own. Regional commanders had received the message from their commander loud and clear. They were to continue as planned. Some leaders questioned the possibility of success without a coordinated attack. They voiced their concerns with Governor Andrews, their new commander.

His response was brief, "We continue with our mission as planned. This is the fight for the soul of our nation. We strike first, we strike hard, we take our country back, so that we can ensure democracy survives today, tomorrow, and every day!"

Doubt of success loomed large on the shoulders of several leaders. There had been little time to train average American citizens with absolutely no combat knowledge. They were severely short on weapons and munitions. Several of their locations were also running low on food and water. They were about to embark on a mission to fight against the greatest military in the world with little preparation or training.

The attack on Washington, D.C. and several federal government sites throughout the nation had yielded significant support in their direction, but it also gave rise to a wave of citizens that felt alienated by the attacks on the homeland. Many of these citizens armed up and headed for their nearest military base to offer their assistance to Vil's forces. The American people had drawn their battle lines.

Days had passed and Governor Andrews had still not heard any word from anyone at the former Sierra Nevada compound. He had to presume they had been lost in the attack. There was no time to send anyone to look for survivors. They had their marching orders and there was no time to waste. He issued the order, on time, to launch the first ground assault by the Freedom Forces.

The attack was launched simultaneously throughout the nation. The Freedom Forces launched the pre-dawn attack on January 28th, just before four o'clock in the morning on the east coast, simultaneously around the nation. They planned to catch Vil's forces off guard by attacking in the middle of the night. Their attack was met by an unprepared military and civilian force caught deeply by surprise.

During the first hours of the attack, they successfully took control of some key sites, including army, air force, naval and submarine bases. They also took control of several strategic government facilities; giving them access to greater control over the nation's power grid infrastructure.

A HOPEFUL SIGN

February 2nd, 2021

A few days into the attacks, word reached Governor Andrews that there were survivors of the Sierra Nevada attack. Five survivors had been discovered by an elderly man out with his dog at a lake east of the former compound.

The governor requested they be brought in immediately and dispatched a rescue team to bring them to his compound, and an undisclosed location outside of Colorado Springs, for questioning and debriefing. He had been so preoccupied with the campaign to quickly overrun Vil's forces that he forgot to inquire the names of the survivors. When they arrived at his compound two days later, he was surprised and pleased when he saw General Hamilton walk in with several other survivors.

"General, it is so good to see that you are alive. Are you okay?" asked Governor Andrews as he embraced the general.

"Yes, everyone in my group made it out and is doing well. When we left the compound, we split into several groups to reduce the chances of being captured. Have you heard any word about Protectorate Perez or Brigadier General Augustus?" asked General Hamilton.

"No, unfortunately we have not heard from them. We were hoping they would have been with you. Do you think they could have been lost in the explosion?"

"I do not think so. We had plenty of time to escape the compound before the attack and they did not use nuclear weapons on the compound, so the destruction appeared to be limited only to the compound itself. They are most likely hiding out somewhere in the mountains waiting to emerge when it is safe. We should send some rescue crews to look for them."

"We have just been incredibly overwhelmed with taking over coordination and keeping the timeline that we do not have anyone to allocate to find them."

"Let me send the other survivors from my team back there to look for them. They will just need some vehicles, plenty of guns and ammo and some rations for a few weeks."

"A few weeks? That seems like a really long time to be looking for survivors. Do you think that is wise to send just a few soldiers to go look for possible survivors? There are hundreds of square miles and you have no idea where to even start looking."

"It is better to be safe than sorry. There is no telling who they may encounter while they are out there but we cannot give up on them. You would want them to come looking for you if the positions were reversed. Yes, they do have a lot of area to cover, but I am confident that if they are out there still then we can find them."

"You are right. Have your team get some rest and I will make sure that they have everything they need by the morning. We should never leave anyone behind. We are all Americans after all, and in due time, we will once again be a reunited nation."

"Yes, they do need a good night's rest and a good meal before they head out in the morning. We will find them; I am sure of it."

"General, another thing; how were you discovered? We were told that you came across an elderly man out in the mountains. Was the man not a Vil sympathizer? How were you able to determine if he was alone? How were you able to contact us?"

"Actually, the man lives east of the mountain range in a small cabin. He told us that he saw the flames, so he decided to go up into the mountains with his dog to investigate. He was worried that the violence had already spread close enough to his home. He thought that living in an isolated location he would be able to avoid any problems, but he had no clue that our headquarters was only miles from his home.

"We came across him when we discovered his car at a lake. We began surveilling him to determine if he was potentially friend or foe. We believed that he was out investigating the noise and smoke and was probably no threat. We were going to send a member of our team down to speak with him. Before one of my soldiers could approach him, his dog sniffed us out and started barking in our direction.

"We decided to come out of the bushes and hope he was alone. He was actually more scared of us because we outnumbered him. At first, he thought we were part of Vil's forces. We told him that we were part of the resistance and that we needed to get in touch with our forces. He was quite relieved to hear that. He offered to take us to his home and use his old CB radio to contact our forces. We are forever in his debt."

"It is great that you came across an American that believes we are on the right side of history. Now, we must bring you up to speed on the current situation as it stands. We will greatly appreciate your military advice now. Over the last few days, we have achieved some major wins and more and more Americans are deciding to join our movement."

THE SPRING OFFENSIVE

Over the next fifteen weeks, the newly branded Freedom Forces made significant battlefield gains against Vil's military and civilian forces. His forces had been woefully unprepared for an attack on the homeland by their fellow Americans. They lacked the intelligence support from the F.B.I, Department of Homeland Security, and Department of Defense after their headquarters had been destroyed weeks earlier. They were unable to defend themselves against the attacks from the Freedom Forces. They were playing defense and on the retreat. How could the greatest military force in the world be defeated by untrained citizens?

Maybe Conrad Augustus had been right after all; they appeared to have history on their side. The momentum was on their side with millions of American citizens joining their ranks to fight for democracy. In a surprising turn of events, they also gained a massive number of military defectors to join their ranks. Hundreds of thousands of servicemembers defected from Vil's forces to join them. They appeared to have awakened to the idea that fighting for the nation meant defeating Vil and removing him for power.

With the growth of these military defectors, they were able to properly train, arm, equip, and send off into the battlefield, a better trained civilian fighting force than they had previously been able to offer. The Freedom Forces were now equipped to bring about a quick end to Vil's reign of power and a quick end to his corrupt government. Governor Andrews was now more hopeful than ever that the end of tyranny was around the corner and they would soon restore civility and normality to a nation that spent the last four years under a corrupt and vile leader who's intentions were not for what was best for the country.

Before the end of the spring offensive, the Freedom Forces had amassed almost total control of a majority of major cities and ports. They decimated much of Vil's forces with little loss of life, took control of major military bases and installations, amassed a massive artillery, and swayed the minds of a sizeable number of citizens that had previously remained undecided or did not want to get involved in the conflict.

CHAPTER 8

AMERICAN CARNAGE

UNDISCLOSED PRESIDENTIAL BUNKER

May 24th, 2021

Fifteen weeks had passed since the beginning of the first major conflict by Americans against Americans since the Civil War. Vil's military appeared to be at a breaking point. How could the greatest military in the world have so quickly succumbed to untrained civilian rebels? Was the greatest military force in the world on the brink of collapse?

Donald Vil would not allow that to happen. It was true, he had fired his top military leaders with the greatest experience only a few months prior. Another series of setbacks came during the first few weeks of the military campaign to remove him from power when he fired several remaining military commanders after a continuous wave of battlefield losses. Almost half of his military fighting force had laid down their arms and joined with the Freedom Forces. His military and civilian forces were in disarray.

Faced with few options that he liked, he turned to a newly promoted rear admiral. Abby Hutchins had recently made a name for herself in the early days of the military campaign. She took command of the U.S.S. Ronald Reagan Carrier Strike Group just days before the naval attack that had been launched on the West Coast. The very next day she ordered the entire strike group to get underway from their naval base in Norfolk, Virginia to project sea power and prevent any ships under her command from being attacked while in port.

She was a woman of small stature, at just over five feet, petite, with pale skin, but a fiery temper. She had built her reputation and naval career for having a bit of a Napoleon complex. This helped her stand out among her male counterparts early in her career and resulted in her being promoted quickly to the one-star flag officer rank of rear admiral lower half, one of the youngest in history.

Once out to sea, she ordered her arsenal of fighter jets from the U.S.S. Ronald Reagan to conduct a counterattack against the Freedom Forces. They were able to slow and prevent gains by the Freedom Forces along certain coastal regions. Her strike group also conducted several missile launches that decimated several Freedom Forces strongholds. The early response from her strike group was praised by President Vil who desperately needed signs of progress to maintain hope.

Abby Hutchins emerged as the new face of Vil's military forces. He promoted her three ranks to become a four-star admiral and gave her total command of all military forces east of the Mississippi River. Her new role required her to have more direct day-to-day oversight of major military operations, which required her to relocate to land.

During the first few days in her new position, she drafted up a plan, in coordination with the other military branches, to push back the Freedom Forces over the course of a several week campaign. They would spread out the factions to isolate them from each other, cut them off from reinforcement and their supply resources, and then get them to surrender. Her plan was vicious, but methodical.

She believed it would take several weeks to accomplish this mission. They had the time and resources at their disposal, and she was ready to draw the mission out as long as it took. The loss of life on either side was not a primary concern for her, she wanted to win, she was tasked to win, and she was known for winning.

SUMMER OFFENSIVE PLAN

June 21st, 2021

Admiral Hutchins moved the military assets under her control into their planned positions for what she believed would be a several weeks-long offensive. The summer heatwave was beginning to hit parts of the country. She believed that gave them an advantage over the Freedom Forces, which consisted mostly of untrained city-dwelling citizens not prepared to fight during intense heat conditions.

She made the extraordinary move of repositioning all U.S. military forces in Europe to assist in the offensive. Under normal circumstances, moving all U.S. military forces out of Europe would have drawn an immediate backlash from allies and praise from Russia. Under the current state of world instability, the European Union held a position to not involve itself in U.S. internal matters.

Russian President Vladimir Porchensky indeed praised the decision of U.S. troop withdrawal. Within days, he amassed thousands of Russian troops on the eastern border of Russia as a show of strength. They started conducting military exercises along the border in preparation for a potential invasion of Europe.

ALLIANCE WITH RUSSIA

June 25th, 2021

Donald Vil had finally accepted that his forces had sustained enough losses that it was time he sought help from President Porchensky. He was confident that the admiral he appointed to oversee military operations east of the Mississippi River would yield back gains on their side. However, he had no control of any of the western states and needed to strike a significant setback to their growing momentum.

Several nations had already publicly called for the president to leave office so peace could return. The United Nations General Assembly publicly denounced the president's actions thus far. But no nation had pledged to interfere with the United States internal affairs.

From a new undisclosed bunker, he contacted the Russian president.

"Vladimir, it has been so long since we last spoke directly without the aid of our military encrypted messages. We have had some major setbacks in the last several weeks that have caused me great concern. We have sustained major setbacks in our fight against these treasonous terrorists. Almost half of my military forces have left to join them. We are fighting a lack of food nationwide because our farmers are not able to maintain their agriculture, our economy is in tatters, and my corporate billionaire buddies are begging me to just walk away from this because it is affecting their wealth.

"I need a major win right now to swing things back in our direction. I have given control of our forces in the east and midwest regions to an admiral that is proving to be a real rightwing military firebrand. But I have lost most of the west to these terrorists. Except for the west coast itself, the region is very wide open, making it hard to locate these groups as they can scatter throughout. I need your help in whatever manner you can assist so we can seize control of this nation again and end this once and for all."

"Have you learned nothing from all of this?" asked President Porchensky. Before Donald Vil could respond, he continued, "If I wanted to see this over anytime soon, I would have intervened several months ago. I am quite content with the way things are moving along. Your military forces and civilian fighters are holding the line. Yes, you have sustained major losses very quickly, but you are beginning to show signs of improvement.

"You have amassed all of your military forces up and down the east coast and presumably in the coming days you will push back these terrorists. If I send my military in to assist you, then we will only serve to eliminate your problem, which will allow America to begin the process of recovery. That is not part of our plan. I have an opportunity to take over Europe and finally make Russia the empire that I have dreamt of my entire life. If I assist you in eliminating your problem, then I have to divert resources away from what I am doing here."

"I understand what you are saying. We both want to see Russia emerge from this as the world leader, but we cannot risk losing over here. What if these terrorists are able to defeat my military and take over control of the nation? At a minimum, we need some assistance to push back their fighters and make them sustain some heavy losses. If nothing else, it can put us in a temporary stalemate while you conduct your operations in Europe."

"Oh, my vision goes well beyond Europe. She is just but the beginning of the plan. I have visions of a Russian Federation that dominates the world!" declared Porchensky.

"Please, whatever help you can give me will allow us to fulfill this plan to take down America once and for all and allow Russia to become great again! We both have the same end goal."

"Here is what I will do for you. We will coordinate together to launch a ballistic missile assault on some enemy locations in the western states simultaneously as you launch your eastern offensive. That should help you enough to put things in a stalemate over there for quite some time."

"That will be a great help to us. It will put some momentum back on our side. However, I am wondering what backlash that will cause for Russia by launching a ballistic missile attack against the United States?" asked Vil.

"Yes, that indeed will be something I have to deal with. But given the current state of world affairs I do not believe it is that much of a problem. Autocrats have been slowly taking over nations and civil wars have been erupting and the world community has done nothing but condemnation. Words mean little anymore. Action is what matters!" commanded Porcensky.

"Indeed, you are right. World leaders do not seem compelled to do anything to stop us autocrats from taking control of nations. It appears that the people of this great planet no longer want to risk their lives to defend what only eighty years ago, their ancestors gave their lives to protect. The people have become so weak. They expect that democracy will always be around and that the way life has been for them is how it will always be."

DIVIDE AND CONQUER

July 4th, 2021 to the end of 2021

In the early predawn hours of July 4th, Admiral Hutchins ordered the start of the counterattack on the Freedom Forces, or what she labeled as the rebel forces. Military aircraft conducted massive raids against the known locations of their enemies. They mounted the largest attack since the beginning of combat operations months prior. In synchronized coordination, the Russian Federation launched a ballistic missile attack on locations on the west coast and Freedom Forces strongholds west of the Mississippi River.

The attacks continued relentlessly for several days. They destroyed several known locations of their enemies. They forced them to splinter and seek refuge from the constant assault. The attacks destroyed their communications network and took out their command center where their leader, Governor Andrews had been located. Countless lives were lost in the few days of the attacks.

After a week of constant strikes, Vil ordered them to stop so they could assess the damage they left on the nation. They had regained control of most bases. Freedom Forces had fled most bases during the first few days of attacks. However, most of the military equipment had already been taken, and the level of destruction done to the bases, rendered them largely useless.

Vil's government had taken back control of the nation's power grids and restored power to several parts of the nation. They assessed that they had killed hundreds of thousands of Americans during the assault, but they would not have a more accurate count for several months. Vil did not care about the loss of life because he considered them all to be traitors. They had refused to recognize him as the one true president and leader of their nation.

Vil decided that he would take the opportunity at hand and attempt to restore the nation to normal. He vowed to see the nation's citizens return to normal society and get the economy and agriculture sector moving once again. He declared victory, while giving his military the authority to roam the streets and seek out anyone they suspected to be traitors.

An era of uncoordinated urban warfare began. Both sides clashed in city streets and in the countryside. Days turned into weeks, and weeks turned into months. The nation was at a stalemate. Some parts of the nation did begin to return to normal living, while most of the nation remained under the threat of assault between the two sides.

The fall months were quickly met with the winter cold. Most fighting had stopped by the time the winter arrived. It became harder and harder for both sides to identify who the enemy was, as both Vil's civilian fighters and the Freedom Forces no longer wore any identifiable military attire. The only fighters left as identifiable to any side were Vil's military forces, which continued to wear their military uniforms.

Vil ordered that anyone caught aiding and abetting the enemy was to be killed on the spot, without a trial.

CHAPTER 9

FREEDOM FORCES

January 1st, 2022

Rosa Perez and Conrad Augustus were running out of breath and freezing in the night cold. They had just escaped the compound where they had been held, along with other members of the Freedom Forces, for the last eleven months. Only seven of the original forty-two in their group survived the eleven grueling months in captivity, and only five of them made it out alive during the escape that night.

"Conrad, it is freezing. We have to find a shelter to get out of this cold. We have been running for what feels like an eternity," wheezed Rosa.

"We have to get as far away from that compound as we can as fast as we can. Those militia members are going to come looking for us as soon as they discover we are gone, which I am sure has already happened. We are in the middle of a damn forest and have no idea where we are, or where the closest city is to us," exasperated Conrad in his exhaustion.

He continued, "Look, you are right Rosa, we need to find shelter to get out of this cold before sunrise, which should be very soon." Turning to the rest of the group, he asked, "In what direction do you guys think we should go?"

They looked at each other with blank faces for several seconds. No one wanted to make a decision that could prove to be the wrong one. Conrad was about to break the silence when a noise in the distance caught his attention.

"Did you all hear that? It sounded like a car. We must not be too far from a road," Conrad declared.

He led the group in the direction of the sound. Soon they came upon a clearing in the brush where they discovered a small farmhouse. After the group weighed the options of approaching the home and what story they would come up with to explain why they were there, they decided that they would split up and approach the home from multiple directions.

Conrad approached the front door as the sun broke through the morning fog. He suddenly felt a sense of calm in him. He had not felt the warmth of the sun in months. He listened for any noise on the other side of the door for a few moments and then shakily knocked on the door.

He heard the sound of what he believed were boots heading in his direction. The noise got louder and louder, then suddenly stopped. The knob turned, giving Conrad a sinking feeling in his heart, while bracing for the worst. A tall, pale skinned, middle-aged woman, appeared at the door opening, holding a shotgun.

"Yes, can I help you?" the woman asked.

"Miss, I am sorry to disturb you, but my friends and I are lost. Our car broke down a few miles back and we were hoping you had power and a working phone we could use to call for some assistance," Conrad lied.

The plan the group had conceived was to gain entry into the home, determine how many people were in the home and get them all in one central location. Then they would distract them to overpower them. Once they had restrained them, they would determine their loyalty, if any, and find a means of contacting one of their close allies.

The woman stared at Conrad for what felt like an eternity to him. He knew she was determining whether he was being truthful with her and why he was out so far away from any major city. His appearance was not well maintained. His beard was long and not kempt, his clothes were tattered, and he looked very pale and malnourished.

Before the woman said a word, the others came around the sides of the house. She felt threatened by the group and clenched harder to her shotgun. Then she saw the one woman in the group. She immediately recognized her as Rosa Perez, the former governor of California and leader of the resistance to remove Vil from power.

"What in the hell is going on here?" asked the woman.

"We do not mean to startle you. We simply need to use your phone and then we will leave," interjected Rosa.

"Stop lying to me!" the woman exclaimed. "I know who you are!"

"We do not mean you any harm. We simply want to get in contact with someone that can help us get back home."

"Home? We thought you were dead. The whole country is in disarray."

Feeling that the woman might be an ally or at least a sympathizer, Rosa asked, "What has happened? Can we trust you?"

"So much has happened since we heard that you went missing. Everyone thought you were dead. How about you all come in out of the cold. You look like you can use a warm breakfast. We have a lot to talk about and you will be safe in here."

The woman took them inside and allowed them to clean up. She cooked them a much needed meal, while bringing them up too speed on what had occurred over the last eleven months since they had disappeared. She explained that the conflict had become a stalemate and that urban warfare was tearing up the cities. The best way she could describe it was to compare it to a third world country in the middle of a several yearslong civil war.

She explained to them that she had no intention of getting involved in the conflict. She had a small farm in Wyoming far from any city. She enjoyed her isolated life.

The last thing she wanted was to disrupt her life to get involved in something that she was not passionate about. Her entire life she saw politicians lie, so she wanted nothing to do with what she believed was a political fight. She was only compelled to take sides after the economy was ruined and her farm failed because of the ongoing conflict. That was when she decided to join the resistance movement. She had never trusted Vil, but only felt the desire to join their side after she reconciled that it was Vil's actions and lies that had led to the conflict in the first place.

After the woman brought them up to speed with the current state of disarray in the ongoing conflict, she told them that she left the fight to come back to her home. She felt that the stalemate was just going to cause needless loss of life and would eventually result in the surrender of the Freedom Forces. Then she turned to Rosa and asked her to explain how they ended up on her farm and to explain where they had been these last eleven months.

"We had received advanced warning that our headquarters was about to come under an air attack, so we packed up what little we could bring with us and fled. There were several hundred of us, so we split up into groups and went in separate directions to increase the chances of survival and reduce the risk of being captured if we made it out alive. We were far away from our headquarters by the time the bombers dropped their arsenal, and we assumed the other groups must have all made it far enough away to avoid the explosions.

"After a few days, we were running low on rations and decided to take a short rest. Well, we made the wrong decision, because we ended up being surrounded by a paramilitary group. They took us hostage, blindfolded us, and transported us for several hours back to their complex.

"They quickly recognized who I was, and they separated me from the others. The rest were interrogated, beaten, and kept in isolation. They used several interrogation tactics on me to get me to break and give up our plans. They waterboarded me, used sleep deprivation tactics, threatened my life, threatened the lives of our team, but they eventually realized I would not break.

"Eventually they decided to hold me ransom and make money from turning me over to Vil. That must have been around the springtime because I remember the weather was starting to warm during the days, but it was still chilly at night. They had already taken the lives of several of our team by then.

"A large convoy of military vehicles arrived, and they took out the paramilitary group. We learned later that they were CIA agents. Vil had sent them to take out the paramilitary members and keep us hostage at that location. Apparently, it was easier to keep us hidden away in an unknown location rather than have any liability for us in public.

"We continued to be interrogated for months. They wanted to know our secret locations and what governments aided us. They were consistent and very well trained in their tactics. We lost several more of our team.

"We all started to individually learn their routines. We would talk to each other whenever the opportunity arose. Everyone left began to learn the layout of the complex once we were taken out of our individual cells more frequently.

"Just a few days ago there seemed to be less guards around the complex. I assumed that maybe it was the holidays and some of them left to go be with their families. The night that we escaped, a guard came into my cell and attempted to sexually assault me. I was able to garner the strength to overpower him. I knocked him out cold by banging his head against the sink.

"I quickly grabbed the cell keys from his pocket and escaped from my cell, locking him inside. I then went through the rest of the corridor and opened the remaining cell doors to the four other survivors that are here with me now. We were able to sneak out of the complex undetected thanks to everyone inside appearing to be drinking and in a celebratory mood."

The woman interjected, "That is probably because they were celebrating the new year. Today is January 1st, 2022."

"We had no idea where we were. We just ran and kept running until we came across your home. We took the chance that we could use your phone and if things did not go well then we might have luck in our numbers."

"Oh that is right, you need to use my phone. Thank goodness the cell towers are working again," the woman said, handing her cell phone to Rosa.

"Who are you going to call, Rosa?" asked Conrad.

"Well, I am hoping that our good friend Mustafa made it to safety after fleeing the headquarters. Hopefully he still has the secure phone I gave him."

Rosa dialed the number to Mustafa's secure phone. She remembered the numbers after the area code because the first three digits matched her home address in California and the remaining four digits was her anniversary. She thought it to be a sign that the numbers were so unique that she could remember them. The phone was making a ringing tone which made her believe that the phone was working.

"Ummm.....hello?" the voice on the other end inquired.

"Is this Mustafa?" asked Rosa.

"Rosa? Is that you?" Mustafa questioned.

"Yes, Mustafa, it is me. Are you safe? Are you in a place we can talk?"

"I am in Montreal, Canada with my family. We escaped the compound and after several months of fighting things took a turn for the worse. We fled to Canada and sought asylum. Rosa, things are not looking good for America. What happened to you? Are you okay? Where have you been all this time?"

Rosa and Mustafa spoke for a lengthy period of time. She explained the events that occurred to her and her group. They spoke about the current situation with the ongoing stalemate between both sides of a fractured nation. She concluded that she would find a way to Canada and attempt to speak with the prime minister to seek aid for their cause.

The woman offered her truck and the group headed north. They drove mostly on back roads to avoid being caught. When they arrived at the border, they veered off the road and found a spot to cross the border in order to avoid being detected.

AN ALLIANCE WITH OUR NEIGHBORS

January 4th, 2022

They arrived in Ottawa, Canada and met up with Mustafa. He had agreed to come from Montreal and offer them help. He had several contacts with some of Canada's most influential politicians and was able to secure a meeting with the prime minister. He was guaranteed only a brief private meeting between the prime minister and Rosa and her team.

The contentious discussion ended up lasting for several hours. At its conclusion, the prime minister agreed to offer military assistance, financial support, and food rations to the Freedom Forces. There was a stipulation attached, the assistance would only happen if she would agree to eliminate all trade barriers between the nations and establish a stronger alliance between the nations if they succeeded.

The decision did not come easy for the prime minister. If the Freedom Forces failed, then the alliance between the two nations would be forever fractured. Unbeknownst to them, he had already received significant pressure from the United Nations to place sanctions on the Vil government for the fury it had unleashed on the American people.

After they left, he reached out to several other allied nations to inform them of the Canadian position. He had been so captivated by the influence and leadership of Rosa Perez that he wanted to convince other nations to stand with the Freedom Forces. He did not want to see Canada's partner to the south fall to tyranny. They would be forever in debt to their allies to the north.

NATION IN TURMOIL

January 6th, 2022

Rosa and Conrad returned across the border after they secured the promise from the prime minister. Now, they had to take back control of the Freedom Forces. They had to unite everyone that stood for American democracy to finally defeat Vil. The task before them was once again daunting, but nothing that was too much for them.

Conrad remembered that they had a location in the Adirondack Mountains of northern New York. If it was still there and still under Freedom Forces control, then they could use it to plan their return and a new offensive. They hiked for three days in the cold until they arrived at the secret location.

Once they arrived, they were surrounded by several individuals in military uniforms with firearms. They did not put up any resistance, were quickly handcuffed, taken into a bunker, and locked up in a large room. It was several hours before anyone came to speak to them. Conrad and Rosa were quite relieved when they saw General Hamilton enter.

"General, what are you doing here? We are so glad to know that you are still alive!" exclaimed Conrad.

"We took you for dead a long time ago. After we fled the old headquarters, we found our way in Colorado where we mounted the resistance for as long as we could," General Hamilton started.

"We were making great gains and pushing back Vil's forces. The momentum was really on our side. We thought we could win this and take back the nation in only a few more weeks. Then, the Russians got involved. They knew where almost all of our strongholds were and completely leveled them. They must have killed over a million Americans during their raids.

"Governor Andrews had me leave the compound to come up here to have better control of our eastern forces. They leveled his compound, and we believe he was lost. These last several months have been brutal. Both sides have resorted to urban warfare, which has brought us to a stalemate. Every day we lose thousands of our fellow Americans. I am not sure how much longer we can continue to sustain this level of fighting.

"We are no longer in control of what is going on at the ground level. Everyone is fighting just out of anger. We do our best to keep spirits alive, but this now appears to be a hopeless fight. The nation seems to be lost."

"It is time that we change that general," Rosa asserted. "We are in the fight for democracy. I want you and Conrad...excuse me, General Augustus to devise a plan to coordinate our forces. If we still have contact with the U.S.S. Franklin D. Roosevelt, it is time we put them to use and get the momentum back on our side. Once you have devised your plan and find a means to get me in front of a camera, then I will once again address the nation. It is time for us to finish what we started and ensure that democracy survives for another generation of Americans."

Protectorate Perez promoted Conrad to the rank of four-star general for the loyalty and leadership he displayed when they were in captivity. She had made him the third in command of the Freedom Forces.

UNCIVIL WAR

January 20th, 2022

Conrad and General Hamilton briefed Protectorate Rosa Perez on the new plan to reunite their forces and defeat Vil. Word was reaching their forces that she was still alive and ready to resume command of the Freedom Forces. Several leadership members of their now splintered forces started to spread the hope that they would now have more assistance to defeat Vil.

It was now time for her to address a nation exhausted from the violence. Conrad had a team go to the closest city's television studio to find and seize a television camera for them. Rosa had prepared her remarks. The coordination with the alliance was now going to be tested. The camera went live.

"My fellow Americans, we once again find ourselves in crisis. Our nation has been torn apart by this fighting. Donald Vil continues to be propped up by his loyalists and with the help of the Russian leader President Vladimir Porchensky.

"There have been challenging times in our nation's history. We have endured wars, economic collapse, acts of terrorism, unjust slavery of other human beings, oppression of certain segments of our population, and a civil war to name just some of our most challenging times. But never have we faced an era where Americans fall victim to a lie, in fact the greatest lie in American history.

"Donald E. Vil lost the presidential election. He fabricated a lie that convinced many of his followers to continue to believe in him. They fell for it because they did not want to lose. It was no longer about doing what is right, it became only about winning. If you fell for his lies, I am now calling on you to look deep into your soul and ask yourself if this is truly what you believe in? Is this really the message you want to tell your children?

"We are a nation at a crossroads. Will we allow this chaos to endure, or will we do what our forebearers did and stand up for justice and righteousness? What legacy will we leave for our children? Are we a people, a society that believes that our greatest days are still ahead of us, or do we believe that we are now in the waning days of our great republic?

"I, for one, believe we have a great burden upon our shoulders. We must stand up to tyranny and take our nation back, for our children, for the world, for of civilization itself.

"Hate at this level can only be sustained for so long before it leads to actual war. That is where we find ourselves at now. We are now entering a new civil war…an uncivil war. We are no longer resisting tyranny; we are fighting for freedom and democracy. We are fighting to secure our future!

"My fellow Americans, join with us so that we can end this uncivil war and make America live up to her ideals and finally make her a great nation!"

AMERICAN ALLIANCE

Shortly after her speech concluded, the Mexican president issued a public pledge that Mexico would support the Freedom Forces. The Canadian prime minister also issued a public statement of support and a pledge to assist the Freedom Forces. Now that they had the support of the nation's neighbors and closest allies, the fight for the nation's soul was theirs to win.